Hubert Hall, Ralph Nevill

The Antiquities and Curiosities of the Exchequer

Hubert Hall, Ralph Nevill

The Antiquities and Curiosities of the Exchequer

ISBN/EAN: 9783742810779

Manufactured in Europe, USA, Canada, Australia, Japa

Cover: Foto ©Andreas Hilbeck / pixelio.de

Manufactured and distributed by brebook publishing software
(www.brebook.com)

Hubert Hall, Ralph Nevill

The Antiquities and Curiosities of the Exchequer

BY

HUBERT HALL, F.S.A.,

Of H.M. Public Record Office, Author of 'A History of the Customs Revenue,' 'Society in the Elizabethan Age,' etc.

WITH ILLUSTRATIONS BY RALPH NEVILL, F.S.A.

AND PREFACE

BY THE

RT. HON. SIR JOHN LUBBOCK, Bart., F.R.S., F.S.A.

LONDON:

ELLIOT STOCK, 62, PATERNOSTER ROW.

1898.

PREFACE.

M R. GOMME proposes, in conjunction with Mr. Ordish, to issue a series of volumes in illustration of Ancient English History, suited to the ordinary reader as well as to the professed antiquary, and he has asked me to write a short preface.

I do not know why I should have been selected, for, although I have no doubt taken a great interest in archæology, it has rather been that of pre-historic times. Perhaps, however, it is partly because my friend, Mr. Gomme, knows that I should wish to do anything he asks me, and partly because I have been for many years a member, and was for some time chairman, of the Public Accounts Committee, and may therefore be supposed to know something of the subject dealt with in the first volume.

This, which is by Mr. Hubert Hall, of the Public Record Office, is devoted to the ' Antiquities and Curiosities of the Exchequer.' It will be followed by others on Old London Theatres, English Homes in the Past, Camden's Britannia, Monastic Arrangement, English Armour, Folk-Lore, Church Plate, Manners and Customs of the English People, Parochial Church-Life in Mediæval England, the Streams of London, Miniature Portrait-painting in England, etc.

The subjects chosen deal with the real history of the nation, which, as is now generally recognised, consists less of the struggles of war than of the events of peace.

The records of the ancient treasury of the kings of England are not only interesting to the Financier, but are enlivened by some quaint yet instructive stories.

For instance, a vivid idea of the primitive British treasury is given by the legend of ' The Thief and the Treasury,' of Edward the Confessor. The national treasure, it appears, at that time was kept in the royal bedroom. One evening, after the king had gone to rest, the anxieties of state kept him awake. Hugo, the chamberlain, comes into the room, takes some money out of the chest, but forgets to lock it up. Shortly after, the scullion of the kitchen, ' in the course of his duties,' enters the royal bedchamber, sees that the treasury is open, and, thinking the king was asleep, seizes as much money as he can carry off. He comes back a second and even a third time, but then the king heard Hugo, and warned the thief :

> ' Fly, fellow, for well I know
> That Hugo the Chamberlain is coming ;
> By the Mother of God, assuredly
> He will not leave you even a halfpenny.'

Scarcely less curious is the story of the great robbery in the reign of Edward I. by Podelicote and the monks of Westminster, who became so reckless that people passing the gates of the Abbey actually picked up silver cups and dishes, gold ornaments and precious stones, and the very fishermen of Battersea brought up silver plate in their nets.

The royal treasure consisted in those times to a considerable extent in plate and precious stones, which in the then state of the coinage could be used in emergencies almost as easily as money.

Richard II. pawned the great crown to the City of London for £4,000.

Mr. Hall gives an interesting account of the famous exchequer table and the curious manner in which the accounts were kept. If the proceedings appear to us absurdly archaic, we must remember that the wooden ' tallies,' on which a large notch represented a thousand pounds, and smaller notches other sums, while a halfpenny was denoted by a small round hole, were actually in use at the Exchequer until the year 1824.

I have in my own possession a 'tally' representing a sum of £24,000, advanced to the Crown by the East India Company.

I must not, however, enter into details, but if the succeeding volumes are as well done as that by Mr. Hall, the series will be both valuable and interesting.

JOHN LUBBOCK.

HIGH ELMS, DOWN, KENT,
July, 1891.

AUTHOR'S PREFACE.

THE Exchequer is in some respects the most characteristic of all our national institutions. It is certainly the stock from which the several branches of the administration originally sprang, and the same motive for its existence, namely, the methodical collection and disbursement of money, will probably be found to underlie the commercial greatness of this country. Just as the Exchequer was the earliest and greatest counting-house in the kingdom, and the undoubted model of all financial operations, baronial or municipal, so still more in the exercise of its control of trade, in the regulation of weights and measures, and, above all, in the maintenance of an unrivalled standard of coinage, it has contributed in an almost immeasurable degree towards the making of England.

It would probably surprise many people to learn that the Treasury Board and the Bank of England are the modern representatives of the

ancient Exchequer, the one representing the former
department of the lord high treasurer, whose hard-
worked deputy, with the successive titles of clerk,
under-treasurer, and secretary to the treasury, is
now one of the most responsible and indispensable
of all the permanent officers of the state ; the
other as representing the clerical functions of the
Receipt and scriptorium, under the supervision of
the chamberlains and marshal. It is true that the
legal department of the Exchequer survives in the
title of a solitary Baron and of a Queen's Remembrancer, who is also reputed the last of his race,
but with the extinction of these two offices of
state, few indeed will remain with an antiquity
earlier than the reign of Edward I., and of these
one is that of the Chancellor of the Exchequer.

Enough has been said here to indicate the importance and interest which attach to the Exchequer
as a national institution. It is in the hope of
drawing attention to the quaint surroundings and
mystical practice of this ancient court that the following pages have been written. This, it is needless to say, has no pretence to be an exhaustive
treatise on the subject of mediæval finance or
legal antiquities. The history of the Exchequer
in this aspect has been already written with greater
show of learning than that bestowed on any single
institution of this or any other country, but at the
same time without being in the least degree intelli-

gible to other than equally learned readers. It has been attempted here to bring together a number of original theories, announced at various times by the author, for the purpose of a reconstruction of the ancient Exchequer, its treasury and house, with their chests and rolls and tallies; its chess-board and game of counters wherein the annual Budget was figured by rude and visible symbols; its working staff, and all the chief appurtenances of its mediæval existence. This account may not be very complete nor its method very enlightened, but at least it was urgently needed to remove the long-standing reproach of a public ignorance of an institution which was before Parliaments, and which will endure after monarchy.

Suppleat igitur defectum meum quicunque voluerit, et ignoscat.

H. H.

London,
  March 24, 1891.

CONTENTS.

CHAPTER VI.

CHAPTER VII.

LIST OF ILLUSTRATIONS.

ANTIQUITIES OF THE EXCHEQUER.

CHAPTER I.

THE ANCIENT TREASURY OF THE KINGS OF ENGLAND.

THE author of the most exact and scientific treatise on the revenue of this or any other country, Richard Fitz-Neale, the king's treasurer, and Bishop of London in the reign of Richard I., when asked by a youthful colleague to define the term 'treasury,' replied, by the Scriptural figure, that it would be found near the heart of its royal owner. The saying was more literally true than at first appears to us, not only on account of the reality of the power of the purse, and of the responsibilities which its possession entailed upon sovereigns who were their own chancellors of the exchequer and paymasters-general, but also because within the strong doors of this jealously-guarded chamber of the royal castle or abbey there were preserved

I

side by side with sacks or money-chests the legal records of the kingdom, which every justice-loving king valued at their true worth, the great seal which has been found indispensable for any form of government, even to an anarchy, and those regalia, robes of state, and other apparatus, whose appearance marked the welcome revolutions of the three great yearly feasts.

Now, the interpretation of the good bishop's parable is this, that the king's treasury would be found constantly near his own person—that is to say, within the recesses of his official residence—only it is by no means easy to identify the particular residence in question before the end of the twelfth century.

The confusion which has always prevailed on this point is almost entirely owing to the practice of old writers of employing the word 'treasury' as a collective term. In truth they went so far as to make 'treasury' and 'treasure' interchangeable words,* or, rather, they used the latter word exclusively in both senses. It is possible, however, to differentiate the term so as to distinguish three distinct receptacles. There was first the king's chamber with its 'hoard,' which is the ancestor of the modern privy purse. Secondly, there was the state treasury, located at some official centre, such

* 'Quod Thesaurus interdum dicitur ipsa pecunia, interdum locus in quo recipitur.'—*Dialogus*, i. 14.

as Westminster or Winchester. Thirdly, there were several more or less permanent but wholly subsidiary treasuries in several provincial towns, and seemingly in the royal castles there. Of these the chamber-treasury* naturally followed the king's progress either abroad or from one hunting palace to another, and although its operations were frequently on a large scale, the bulk of treasure was necessarily limited by the exigencies of mediæval conveyance, so that payments for the king's service were usually made by an elaborate system of assignment. This was effected in the following way : During the king's progress the personal requirements of himself and his courtiers were provided for by means of orders upon the provincial officers, who in turn were allowed upon their annual accounts for supplying so many quarters of grain or bacons, for clothing and armour, and even for building operations or the entertainment of royal visitors. Indeed, for half a century after the Conquest there could have been very little need of a central treasury at all, since the greater part of these provisions formed an intrinsic portion of the revenue itself—that is to say, the beeves and bacons and corn which maintained good cheer at the court, and thus accounted for a large part of the royal expenditure, were not paid for by the sheriff or bailiff, but collected or

* *Camera curiæ.*

I—2

advanced as an instalment of the revenue, which was still payable in kind. This point is both important and interesting, and has been hitherto somewhat overlooked by economic writers. The fact (which is probable in itself) rests on high authority—that of the famous treasurer of the first two Plantagenet kings ; but when the utmost allowance has been made for the consuming powers of the royal household, it will be evident that the surplus revenue must eventually have been amassed and dealt with in some other way. It is at this point that the central treasury in the principal palace of the Saxon and Norman kings comes into play, supplemented for convenience of collection or distribution by the provincial treasuries before alluded to.

The king's Palace of Westminster appears to have possessed such a central treasury even before the Conquest. There is no official record of this fact, but the descriptive hints gathered from the work of a monk of Westminster, writing within a century of its reputed existence, may be fairly held to have been inspired by a local tradition. The writer in question is Osbert, Prior of Westminster in the reign of Henry II., whose ' Life and Miracles of the Confessor ' formed the basis of the better-known work of Ailred of Rievaulx, and the metrical ' Life ' of the next century. In the version last named we have several most interesting notices of a treasury at Westminster. There was here a ' hoard,' situated, according to a custom which long survived, in the actual bedchamber of the sovereign. A good idea of the extent and use of this primitive department may be obtained from the following legend of ' The Thief in the Treasury :'

LEGEND OF THE THIEF IN THE TREASURY.[*]

' One day it came about by chance,
   After much counsel and care,
   Lying on his bed he could not sleep,
   Nevertheless he reposed himself,
   And supported his drooping head.
   Now arrived Hugelin
   The chamberlain, who takes some money,
   Carries off as much as he wished
   To pay to his seneschals,
   To his caterers and marshals,
   But in his haste he forgets
   That he shuts not the chest.
   The scullion of the kitchen
   Goes to do his office,
   Well believes that asleep is
   The king, and seizes the money.
   He goes to conceal them, and then returns,
   And takes as much and conceals them at once.
   And a third time, for he had no fear
   Of Hugelin, who delays for long,
   He desires to take a large portion of the money.
   The king sees all, who is not asleep,
   Who in spirit sees that quickly

* From Dr. Luard's translation in the ' Life of Edward the Confessor' (Rolls Series).

> Afterwards there the officer would come,
> And says, "Fly, fellow, for well I know
> That Hugo the chamberlain is coming;
> By the Mother of God, assuredly
> He will not leave you even a halfpenny."
> He departed without speaking a word;
> The king gives him leave to go in peace.
> The chamberlain afterwards returns,
> And sees at a glance the theft,
> By a great mark which he finds there,
> Proves that the injury has been done there.
> He sees the diminution,
> And perceives that the king is awake;
> Then like one astonished he cries out
> " Harro !" but the king rebukes him.'

Besides this treasury of the chamber, there is evidence of a regular treasury also, apparently, at Westminster. Another legend of the Confessor's life describes his inspection of this chamber under the guidance of his treasurer, and mentions ' large and full barrels' of money ranged round the walls, on one of which the king perceived a devil seated, a sight which confirmed him in his dislike of those financial processes which were even then beginning to lay the foundations of the power of the purse. Therefore, he remitted the Danegeld; but even without this source of revenue, we read that :

> ' With gold and silver he was provided,
> And thus was much more feared.'

Harold, on the other hand, is described, characteristically, by the monkish biographer as delighting in this increase of the revenue:

' Money he amasses like a usurer,
  To despoil his people he ceases not.
  Like a justice at the treasury
  He sits to count the money.'

This last picture of the royal treasury as an organized department of the state is very striking, and it may fairly be compared with the similar practice in vogue during the reign of Henry I., or even earlier, when the sheriffs' accounts were audited, and other business transacted, at the central treasury, as distinguished from the peripatetic *curia*.

One more passage of this metrical history may be quoted in proof of the official importance of Westminster, as well as for the sake of the suggestion contained therein that this central treasury may have been situated in the abbey rather than in the palace itself.

'And the church at Westminster,
  Which has no equal in the kingdom
           *   *   *
  And it has the dignity of the *regalia*,
  Whence I say it has no equal.'

Westminster appears thus early as the official residence (so to speak) of the English kings, and this position was improved rather than diminished during the next century. The Confessor's palace, itself an innovation upon native architecture, was extended by the ambition or policy of his Norman successors, and it is important to notice that this

extension took the form chiefly of apartments of
state, the great hall of Rufus, that· is to say, and
those buildings adjacent which have been used
from time immemorial for official purposes. Of
course it is quite possible that this official aspect
of the ancient palace may be a purely secondary
one ; that the great hall was designed simply as a
banqueting-house, and that the exchequer-house
(if it then existed at all) was a lean-to structure in
the nature of a domestic office.   In any case the
treasury would at first have been situated within
the interior of the palace, or, according to an alternative theory, within the cloisters of the adjacent
abbey.

Although Westminster possessed an irresistible
attraction to a pious sovereign through the
vicinity of a favoured church, Norman kings ,
engrossed in the pleasures of the chase, and
constantly embroiled in Continental wars, found
the ancient Saxon capital of Winchester better
adapted for the pursuit of sport as well as for
the maintenance of their foreign communications
through the proximity of the great mediæval seaport, Southampton.   It is probable, therefore, that
for the next fifty years at least the royal treasury,
with the regalia and records, were deposited here
more or less permanently in the treasury of the
royal castle.   There was formerly a tradition of
this treasury having been situated in the church,

chiefly owing to the fanciful derivation of the title of 'Domésday Book' from *Domus Dei*, this national record having been always preserved in the royal treasury. It is certainly true that the word is once written thus by a twelfth-century scribe, but the church in question would more probably have been that of Westminster, and in any case the etymology is a false one. A very interesting narrative of a trial which took place in the treasury at Winchester Castle is preserved in the chronicle of Abingdon, which clearly proves the existence of a central department of revenue there between the years 1108 and 1113.*

The tradition of an earlier age has fixed the site of the treasury of the kings of England at Westminster equally with Winchester, and with this treasury the same tradition connects the first germ of an audit of the revenue. The subject is one of great difficulty, arising from the obscurity of description which characterizes contemporary references to date and scene of action, but it is at least possible to evolve a reasonable theory in explanation of the conflicting evidence of a treasury existing at more than one centre during the reign of Henry II.

In the first place we must remember that the treasury as a department of the re-organized

---

* 'Chronicles of Abingdon,' ii. 115-6, quoted by Mr. J. H. Round in the *Antiquary*, July, 1887.

Exchequer was nominally bound to follow the king's progress from one city or hunting-palace to another. We actually find the chief contents of the treasury—bullion, plate or regalia, and records—moved, on several occasions, with great labour and at a heavy expense, from Westminster or Winchester to the temporary abode of the court, or even beyond sea.

The explanation of this inconvenient practice is, probably, to be found in the purely personal nature of this establishment, which, like the king's court, had, as we have seen, its first origin in the informal session of the household officers in the very chamber of the palace. In the course of a century, however, this crude system had been so far refined upon that the treasury had now an independent existence at two permanent centres. The court or Exchequer, being unincumbered with official baggage, could meet in one palace as well as another, while the personal or immediate wants of the king were supplied out of the chamber-treasury, as of old. But it would still happen on certain occasions, usually connected with warlike operations, and as late as the reign of the third Edward, that the whole ' plant ' of the Exchequer and the treasury with it was removed to some distant city. Otherwise, however, the royal treasure was both hoarded and audited at Westminster or Winchester, and the only important point is which of these two cities should be regarded as the official seat of the central treasury.

As the question which arises here can only be decided by reference to contemporary notices gleaned from the few surviving records of the period, it will be more convenient to arrange these brief entries in tabular form, so that the reader will be able to see at a glance the normal position of the treasury down to the close of the reign of Henry II.:

NOTICES OF THE POSITION OF THE KING'S TREASURY BEFORE AND DURING THE REIGN OF HENRY II.

1052—1066. Legends connected with the life of the Confessor, surviving from the twelfth century, which refer to a treasury at Westminster.

1066—1154. Tradition pointing to the existence of a treasury in the palace and abbey there.

1066—1154. Archæology of the above buildings confirming the statement as to their antiquity.

1066—1154. William I., Henry I., Stephen, and Henry II., crowned at Westminster.

1100—1154. The king's treasury at Winchester in 1100, 1108-1113, and 1135.

1130. The ministry of the king's treasury at Winchester held by Geoffrey de Clinton.

1141. Siege of Winchester during the civil wars. The treasure and records probably conveyed to Westminster for safety.

1155. Repairs to the Exchequer nouses at Westminster.

1155. Grant of office and payments to Roger, Usher of the treasury at Westminster.

1155. Pardon to Gervase of the treasury at Winchester.

1156. Treasure conveyed to Cricklade and beyond
sea from Winchester.

1156. Treasure conveyed to Shoreham and beyond
sea from Westminster.

1157. Regalia conveyed to St. Edmunds and beyond
sea from Winchester.

1158. Treasure conveyed to Carlisle and beyond
sea from Winchester.

1158. Regalia (and tallies) conveyed to Worcester
from Winchester.

1158. Wax conveyed to Clarendon from Winchester.

1158. Tallies conveyed to Westminster from Winchester.

1159. Treasure conveyed beyond sea from Winchester.

1160. Treasure conveyed (from the Exchequer) to
Winchester.

1161. Record chest conveyed to London from Winchester.

1161. Treasure conveyed beyond sea from Winchester.

1162. Treasure conveyed beyond sea from Winchester.

1162. Payment to Roger Usher of the treasury at
Westminster.

1162. Records conveyed from Hertford to Westminster.

1162. Treasure conveyed to Southampton and London
from Winchester.

1162. Wax for the summonses provided at Winchester.

1162. For conveying the Danegeld to or from Winchester.

1163. For conveying treasure to or from Winchester.

1163. Plate conveyed to Berkhampstead for Christmas from Winchester.

164. Record chest conveyed to London (Easter)
from Winchester.

1164. Record chest conveyed to Northampton (Michaelmas) from Winchester.

1164. The Exchequer held at Westminster (Michaelmas).

1165. Treasure conveyed to various places from Winchester.

1166. Treasure conveyed to various places from Winchester.

1169. Treasure conveyed to Southampton from Winchester.

1170. Treasure (and regalia) conveyed to Southampton from Winchester.

1170. The treasury chest conveyed from Wycombe to Westminster.

1170. Treasure, records, tallies, and regalia conveyed from Winchester.

1170. The Exchequer held at Winchester.

1171. Treasure chests conveyed from London to Winchester.

1172. Treasure conveyed during the whole year from Winchester.

1173. Treasure conveyed back to Winchester from Southampton.

1173. Treasurer's clerk sent abroad with treasure.

1173. Treasure conveyed to Normandy *and back*.

1173. Treasure conveyed to Winchester and elsewhere from Westminster.

1174. Treasure conveyed to Winchester and elsewhere from Westminster.

1174. Treasure (and hawks, etc.) conveyed during the whole year from Winchester.

1174. The clerk of the chamber and sergeants of the treasury sent abroad with treasure from Winchester.

1175. Treasure conveyed to Gloucester from Westminster.

1176. Treasure returned to London.
1176. Charter dated at the Exchequer at Westminster.
1177. The treasury and records established at Westminster.
1177. Treasure conveyed from London to Winchester, and from Winchester to Clarendon and Porchester and back to London.
1177. Easter Exchequer at Westminster.
1177. Treasure conveyed to Winchester and back to London.
1177. Treasure conveyed to Winchester from Westminster.
1177. Treasury at Winchester repaired.
1179. Treasure conveyed to London from Winchester.
1179. Treasure conveyed to Winchester from Westminster.
1179. Plate conveyed to Southampton from Winchester.
1179. Treasure conveyed after the king from Westminster.
1180. Treasure conveyed to Woodstock from Westminster.
1180. Dies conveyed from Westminster and returned.
1180. Treasure conveyed to London from Winchester.
1180. Treasury implements purchased at Winchester.
1180. Exchequer at Westminster, Michaelmas.
1180. Treasure sent out from Westminster to different mints throughout England to be recoined and returned there.
1181. Plate sent out from Westminster.
1181. Treasure conveyed to Winchester, where the king kept Christmas.
1183. Exchequer at Westminster.
1184. Exchequer at Westminster.
1184. Charter dated at the King's Chapel at Westminster.

1185. Treasure conveyed throughout England from Westminster.

1185. Plate conveyed throughout England from Westminster.

1185. Treasure now sent direct to Southampton.

1186. Treasure now sent direct to Southampton.

1186. New furniture for the Winchester treasury.

1187. The swords of the Winchester treasury furbished.

1187. Treasure conveyed abroad from Winchester.

It is evident from the description of the author of the *Dialogus*, himself the king's treasurer, that the Exchequer and the treasury were both at one centre. In the first place, this treatise was written in a certain apartment of the king's palace at Westminster, close to the site occupied by the Exchequer from time immemorial. In the second place, there are numberless allusions in the body of the work to a treasury situated in close proximity to this Exchequer. Thirdly, we know that there were Exchequer *houses* at Westminster so old as to be in need of repair at the accession of Henry II. Finally, there is the unique evidence of a suitor of the period, verified by the Pipe Rolls, that he paid certain sums into the Treasury of the Receipt of the Exchequer in the eleventh year of this reign, and it can be shown by a curious coincidence that he made these payments at Westminster; while only a few years later we find in the Pipe Rolls the first of a regular series of payments for furniture for the Exchequer out of the farm of London.

Moreover, this Westminster treasury was no secondary or temporary structure, but the fixed receptacle of the treasure-chests, records, and great seal, therefore obviously the principal treasury of the kingdom. It is necessary to enlarge upon these simple facts, because the very existence of this early treasury has been absolutely and authoritatively denied.

It will be gathered from the above table that there was undoubtedly a central treasury still existing at Winchester. The *Dialogus* informs us that tellers of the treasure were constantly employed there. In fact, they were merely summoned to Westminster during the sessions of the Exchequer to assist the resident staff in the work of counting the incoming revenue, their services being subsequently required at Winchester for the purpose of paying out the large drafts transmitted thither for the expenses of the court or camp. Winchester may thus be regarded as an emporium in connection with the transport of bullion (and especially of the regalia and plate), as well as other supplies, *viâ* Southampton or other seaports, to the Continent, during the almost incessant wars of the first twenty years of the reign. After the great rebellion of 1173-4, however, a change of practice seems to have taken place, coinciding with the reorganization of the Curia and Exchequer in the interests of the crown, and the prominence of the official element, with its permanent head-quarters henceforth at Westminster. Similarly, with the renewal of the war, at the close of the reign, the treasury at Winchester was once more largely utilized ; but, having fallen into decay, it required certain structural repairs and a new plant, while the treasury swords actually required to be cleansed of the rust which they had contracted during the ten years or more that the chamberlains and clerks had been in permanent residence at Westminster.*

It must be remembered, in connection with the term ‘ treasure,’ that two different species of bullion were included therein, namely, coin and plate, including regalia and jewels. It is most probable, therefore, that both species were separately hoarded (as they undoubtedly were a century later), and that the Winchester treasury was specially designed to accommodate the latter, until the close of the twelfth century, after which date a permanent repository was provided for them in

* These swords, which were used on occasions of state, may have been returned from Westminster after the coronation of the younger Henry, in 1170, to Winchester, since they were preserved there in 1187. The same remark applies to crowns and plate, etc.

the Abbey of Westminster. The coined treasure, on the other hand, was throughout received and hoarded at Westminster, in the treasury of the Receipt of the Exchequer, in company with the great seal and records, being drafted thence as required into the local treasuries, the king's chamber, or, a generation later, the Wardrobe. This will account for no mention being found of regalia or plate in the treasury described in the *Dialogus*, and agrees with the notices of regalia issued from and returned to Winchester in the Pipe Rolls. We shall see presently that the entire contents of the treasury of the Wardrobe in Westminster Abbey, later, in the reign of Edward I., consisted of regalia, plate, and jewels.

During the king's absence in Scotland, in the years 1301 to 1303, the royal palace seems to have been left, as usual, in the custody of a caretaker, who, according to a custom at least as ancient as the beginning of the reign of Henry II., was also the keeper of the Fleet Prison. There should also have been the ushers of the two Exchequer houses in residence during the vacation or absence of the court, for we know on the authority of a record of a few years' later date,* that the Barons formally committed the custody of these premises to the above subordinate officers at the end of every term, with directions for the safe-keeping of

---

* L. T. R. Memoranda, 5 Edward II.

their contents. In the present instance, however, owing to the transfer of the Exchequer to York, the keeper of the palace, with his servants, was in sole charge. Now, the treasury of the Receipt containing the chests of coined money and records being, as we have seen, attached to the Exchequer, the remaining treasure, which comprised an accumulation of historic jewels, the regalia, and the sumptuous plate used for the service of the king's chapel and table, seems to have been deposited in another treasury, situated within the precincts of the adjacent abbey. Possibly, indeed, some such treasury had been in use for a similar purpose since the days of the Confessor. About four years previous to the date of the following narrative an ugly rumour had been spread of an attempt to break into this treasury, an incident which was further reported to have been hushed up through the intercession of the abbot. No more was heard of the matter, and the king seems to have set out from London in August of the year 1302, leaving a treasure valued at more than £100,000 virtually in the custody of the monks of Westminster, whose late abbot had, it is only fair to say, held the post of treasurer. What occurred during the next eight months will never be precisely known, but some time in the month of May following it began to leak out that persons whose business or curiosity took them within the gates of the palace and abbey had for some time past been picking up silver cups and dishes, gold ornaments and precious stones, round the walls of the palace, and in the cemetery adjacent to the chapter-house and to St. Margaret's Church. The very fishermen of Battersea brought up silver plate in their nets. These lucky finds were passed from hand to hand, often for a few pence. Receivers of such treasure-trove have never been wanting in any age, and soon the stores of half the goldsmiths in London were glutted with what were discovered by inquisition to be the principal contents of the royal treasury. At length news of these strange proceedings reached the ears of the king, who was then at Linlithgow. He at once despatched a writ to four trusty officers to inquire into the circumstances of the robbery, secure the treasure-trove, and arrest the guilty persons. This was on June 6, 1303. The commissioners set to work without delay, and an inquiry was commenced on a more extensive scale than probably was ever attempted in a criminal case during the Middle Ages.

In the first place, on Wednesday after the Octave of St. John the Baptist, ten juries from the wards of the City were assembled at the Bishop of London's hospice, and stated their knowledge of the matter on oath. On the same day a jury of goldsmiths and the aldermen of London were assembled at the Guildhall for a similar purpose. On the Friday following six juries of the county of Middlesex and two juries of Westminster made similar presentations in Westminster Hall. Seven juries of Surrey were assembled at Southwark on the following day, together with the boatmen of the Thames. Other juries from the neighbourhoods of Westminster and Fleet Street were convened at the Temple at Lammas-tide. The palace officers were also separately examined at a later date. As the result of these presentments, a large number of persons were committed to the Tower and other prisons, on grave suspicion of complicity with the perpetrators of the robbery, including a certain pedlar believed to be the principal culprit, the keeper of the palace, the subprior, cellarer and sacristan of the abbey, seven monks, six lay brethren, ten merchants of London, and several women of ill-fame. In addition to this the abbot, with other officers of the abbey, and several others, were compelled to find sureties. The broken plate and jewels already recovered were scheduled and placed for safety in the Tower, Guildhall, and Wardrobe.

In accordance with a further mandate of the crown, dated November 10, a final inquiry was held by several of the king's justices, and the several juries already convened were once more brought up in January of 1304.

Their presentments were very much to the same effect as on the former occasion, revealing an almost incredible state of corruption and laxity of morals on the part of the king's officers and of the monks.* The jurors promptly convicted the pedlar above-mentioned, Richard de Podelicote by name, a desperate character, in whose possession a large part of the stolen treasure had been found. They also grievously suspected the monks of Westminster and the officers of the palace of being accessories to the deed. Moreover, they by no means neglected this favourable opportunity of getting rid of a number of bad characters in the neighbourhood without any further presumption of guilt than that such persons were quite capable of any crime.

The theory of the robbery of the treasury as it was painfully, not to say enigmatically, expounded by these honest lieges is briefly this:

The monks of Westminster, and more particularly certain domestic officers of the abbey, had for long past designed this robbery, as was proved by the attempt previously hushed up, and the theft of a large sum deposited in their hands in connection with the obsequies of the late queen.

---

* The best account of these proceedings is given in his admirable ' History of Crime,' by Mr. L. O. Pike, the present learned editor of the ' Year Books,' or Law Reports of this period.

Having tampered with William of the palace, the keeper, and his fellow officers, a deep-laid plot was successfully carried out for preventing interruption or subsequent discovery. The gates of the palace and Abbey precincts were closed before the usual hours, and public traffic was stopped on frivolous pretences. A daring ruffian (Podelicote) had been secured, and provided with tools by a friendly mason. They had even taken the precaution to sow the ground near the point of attack with hemp, to conceal the traces of their operations, and secure the plunder until such time as it could be safely removed. Many of the neighbouring residents could bear witness to the strange proceedings within the palace walls. The keeper, deserting his wife and home at the Fleet, revelled late at night in the palace grounds in the doubtful companionship of the daughter of Nicholas the cook, while not a few of the good fathers were reported to have kept him company, and ladies were certainly of the party. At the end there was a general scramble to conceal the booty. Monks were seen dropping down their abbey mill-stream with a boatload of mysterious hampers. Hosts and courtesans and usurers were freely plied with cups and platters of silver. An immense quantity of treasure was buried in the cemetery or concealed in the convenient hemp-bed. Some pieces were even found lying beneath the palace walls, and a small quantity fell into the hands of the deserving poor of St. Margaret's. Even the cross of Gneith (a relic which the king regarded with superstitious reverence, and which had a keeper assigned to it from the royal household) was not spared. The subjects whose money had for the last ten years been squeezed from them by the royal exactions now got it back with interest. The beginning of the end seems to have been the discovery made by a worthy chaplain of derelict plate in the very yard of the palace. Then the final scramble took place, and William of the palace had barely time to conceal his share of the plunder under his bed before he was arrested with the other suspects.

The several juries are so unanimous in the above version of the affair that it is scarcely possible to doubt their verdicts, especially in view of the declared ill-fame of certain of the monks, and the lamentable dissensions and recriminations that prevailed in the monastery a year or two later.

Another version, however, exists, which is nothing less than the confession of Podelicote himself. His narrative, which is singularly explicit, completely exonerates the officials, equally with the monks, from any active participation in the robbery. It will be observed that the case against the supposed accessories really amounts only to a charge of unlawful possession, and as the annals of crime present us with numerous instances of successful enterprises of this kind having been effected single-handed by very daring and skilful felons, there is nothing to prevent us from giving a certain credit to his statement, premising, however, that facilities were afforded by the cynical indifference of the officials, who, in the spirit of the wreckers and treasure-seekers of a far later age, thought it no sin to profit by the misadventures of others, especially when the crown was the sufferer.

THE CONFESSION OF RICHARD DE PODELICOTE.*

'He says that he was a travelling merchant of wools, cheese, and butter, and was arrested in Flanders for the king's debts in Brussels, and there was taken from him xivˡ. xviiˢ. in pollards for wools taken for the king's use, for the which he sues in the court of the King of England, at the beginning of August, in the thirty-first year [of Edw. I.], at Westminster; and at that time he espied the state of their refectory of the abbey, and saw betimes how the serjeants there carried in and out hampers of silver, and dishes, and mazers. So thought he then how he might come at the goods that he saw, for that he was poor through the loss he had in Flanders. So he spied about the premises of the abbey everywhere. And on the same

* The narrative is translated here from the Norman-French of the original record.

day that the king departed thence where he tarried towards Barnes, the night following the said Richard—according to what he had espied—found a ladder standing against a house, which was being roofed, close to the palace-gate, over against the abbey, and put this ladder against a window of the chapter-house that opened and shut by a cord, and entered, swinging himself down by the same cord, and from thence went to the door of the refectory and found it close-locked, and with his knife opened it, and entered within, and found six hampers of silver in an aumbry behind the doors, and dishes of silver (thirty or more) in another aumbry, and the hampers containing drinking-cups beneath a bench, all packed together, and carried them all off, and closed the doors after him without locking them. Then of the feet of the cups, and the dishes, and hampers of silver he made his sale, and spent that, even before Christmas next following, and then his money failed, so thought he how he might come to break into the king's treasury. And for that he knew the premises of the abbey, and where the treasury was, and how he might come at it ; so he began eight days before Christmas to enter to make a breach there with implements which he had provided for that purpose ; that is to say, two tarriers (one large, the other small), and knives, and many other engines of iron. And thenceforth he was engaged in breaking in under cover of night, whenever he could discern and see his point, from eight days before Christmas to the Quinzime of Easter following. That then for the first time he entered on a Wednesday night, the Eve of St. Mark, and the whole of St. Mark's Day he remained inside, and arranged that which he wished to carry away. And that which he carried away he carried the night following outside, and of this he left part outside the breach till the next night following, and the remainder he carried with him as far as without the gate behind the Church of St. Margaret, and placed it beneath the wall without the gate, covered with a heap of earth—about twelve pitchers, and in every pitcher he put some jewels, and cups standing and covered. Besides this, he put a great pitcher with precious stones and a cup in a wooden shrine. Besides this, he put three pouches full of jewels and vessels, whereof one was filled with cups, as well whole as broken. In the other was a great crucifix and jewels, a case of silver, with gold dishes. In the third, cups, plates, and nine saucers, and an image of Our Lady of silver-gilt, and two little pitchers of silver. Besides this, he carried to a ditch outside the mews a pot and a cup of silver. Besides this, he carried away with him dishes, saucers, plates of silver for spices, a crown cut up, rings, clasps, precious stones, crowns, belts, and other jewels, which afterwards were found in his possession for the most part. And this same Richard says that, when he took these out of the treasury, he carried them straightway without the gate, close to the Church of St. Margaret, in the cemetery of the Church of St. Margaret, without leaving anything behind him within that gate.'

There are probably few subjects of archæological interest upon which such absolute misconception has hitherto prevailed as in respect of the identity of the treasury mentioned in this robbery. In the first place, older writers, from the sixteenth century onwards, were under the belief that the robbery was committed in the treasury of the Receipt, situated on the east side of the palace, and that the rebuilding of the Exchequer houses in this reign was due to that outrage. Modern writers, on the other hand, have ignored the existence of the Exchequer treasury entirely, supposing that the abbey repository was alone used for the custody of treasure. Thus, Mr. Harrod* missed the point of his strongest argument by insisting that the Exchequer treasury could not have been exposed to attack during four months, since the officials must have been in the habit of visiting it almost daily. As a matter of fact, the king's great treasury in the cloisters (now the Chapel of the Pyx) was not the working treasury of the Exchequer, which was

* *Archæologia*, vol. xliv., part 2.

situated in the Exchequer buildings beyond the
palace ; and, in any case, it is well known that the
Exchequer was at York during the whole of the
period. Neither is it sufficient to assume, as Mr.
Harrod has done, that the treasury of the Wardrobe was normally situated beneath the chapter-
house. It was there undoubtedly in the nineteenth
year and later, but the older and more important
treasury of the Wardrobe was still existing in the
Tower, while there was certainly another in the
palace itself. The greater part of the crown jewels
can be traced, in course of frequent transfers from
one treasury to another, between the king's departure for Scotland and the commission of the
robbery. The real proof of the identity of the
treasury of the Wardrobe with the treasury robbed
in 1303 is found in another document, the narrative of the first discovery of the crime by the
keeper of the Wardrobe himself. This worthy
had been absent since August in the king's business—that is to say, he was apparently employed
in negotiating loans with foreign merchants or
religious houses on the security of the crown
jewels and plate in his custody. On June 20,
1303, he arrived in London on important business,
which seems to have had reference to an intended
pawn of plate with the Friars Minors. The
robbery had just then been discovered, and was
reported to him, whereupon, after submitting his

keys of office in their sealed pouch to the scrutiny of the king's justices, he proceeded in company with the latter, the lord mayor, the warden of the Tower, the prior of Westminster, and several monks, and the cofferer of the queen's Wardrobe, to the scene of the crime. The doors of the treasury were opened, and the damage was at once revealed. Now, this narrative affords positive proof that the treasury in question was not the Exchequer treasury, the keys of which were in the custody of the treasurer and chamberlains. More-over, the description of the contents of this treasury points to the Wardrobe, and not to the Exchequer, as the department in charge.

On the other hand, we have the positive state-ment in the official inquiry that this very treasury (Mr. Harrod has not observed the identity) was broken into on a former occasion from the cloister side, and this would seem to indicate the Chapel of the Pyx, which might easily have been attacked from the close without disagreement with the several surroundings mentioned in the record of inquiry, such as the cemetery of the monks, the hemp-sown grass-plot, the monk's lodging over against the breach, the passage of the bell-ringers, etc. However, it is possible to explain this apparently conflicting statement by the supposition that the vault of the chapter-house was attacked at the threshold of the door leading to the cloisters.

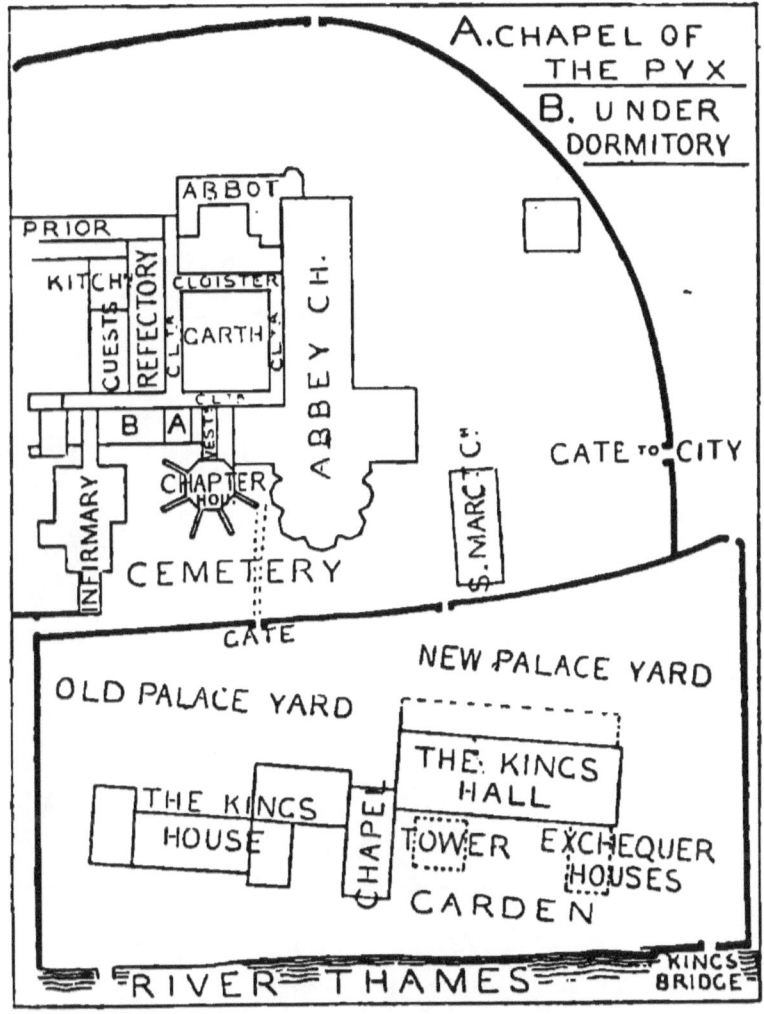

Fig. 1.—Sketch plan of the Palace and Abbey precincts, Westminster.

One peculiar circumstance has hitherto escaped notice, namely, the close connection between this outrage and the rather discreditable methods adopted by the king for raising money. It will be observed that Podelicote himself was a victim, and it is just possible that the wrongs of other merchants and mortgagees may have had more to do with this unexampled contempt of majesty than we are yet aware of.

The result of the inquiry held by the king's officers (Podelicote's confession being apparently ignored) sealed the fate of the principal suspects, several of whom were hanged, while others remained in prison for several years, and among these the monks of Westminster, whose treatment was loudly denounced by contemporary historians of their own order.

It would seem that after this deplorable incident the royal treasury in the cloisters of the abbey was henceforth used as the principal depository of the plate and regalia, which, however, were sometimes lodged in the Tower, and to a less extent in the Wardrobe, while not long afterwards a new department was erected for their better custody, the Jewel-house, which still had one of its centres within the abbey precincts, in a tower situated at the south-western angle of the palace, and which was acquired by the crown from the abbot and convent for this purpose.

From this time onward it is possible to distinguish four separate treasuries at Westminster, all of which were appropriated for the custody of coined money and records. The chief of these was still the great treasury within the cloisters of Westminster Abbey. Here the king's crowns, four in number, and the other regalia, were usually deposited, together with many valuable jewels and records, certairly as late as the reign of Henry VI. Before the close of Elizabeth's reign the jewel-house in the Tower had become the official repository of the regalia and the historic jewels of the crown, being also at this time in the custody of the master of the jewel-house and his subordinates, instead of in that of the treasurer and chamberlains of the Exchequer.

The second treasury was one perhaps equally ancient, but probably less suited for the safe custody of a mass of uncoined treasure. This was the treasury of the Receipt of the Exchequer, and was situated apparently in the lower part of the Exchequer-house, on the east side of the new palace. In the reign of Elizabeth, however, after many additions had been made to the original structure, we learn that a considerable amount of treasure was allowed to lie in chests in the upper part of a building which was now exclusively devoted to the business of the receipt and issue of the revenue.

The third treasury, which was of more modern date, was situated over the little gatehouse of the new palace. The fourth treasury was in the refectory of the abbey, and was probably the private treasury of the abbot and convent, and identical with the strong-room broken into by Podelicote in August of 1302.

From the end of the sixteenth century the four treasuries at Westminster were chiefly used as repositories of records. In fact, the great treasury in the cloisters was frequently termed the treasury of leagues, because the ancient diplomatic records of the kingdom were preserved there. Moreover, all these treasuries were fitted with presses for the records, and the old money-chests were utilized for the same purpose, but the contents of the treasury of the Receipt seem to have remained the same as they were in the time of Richard Fitz-Nigel, and here the keys of the treasury in the abbey were always deposited. The latter chamber is well known to visitors of the abbey as a vaulted room or chapel beneath the old dormitory of the monks, in the cloister next the chapter-house.

The ancient treasury within the Tower of London may fairly be reckoned as a fifth repository of plate, jewels, and records. There was also an inner chamber here, 'next the Black Hall,' and 'under the Great Hall,' which was used for the same purpose from the reign of Edward III., or even earlier.

It is probable that a considerable amount of bullion was periodically stored in the mint, both in the central mint, in the Tower of London, which was erected as a distinct department from the treasury, in the third year of Elizabeth, and in several provincial cities. Still larger sums must have been received in another fiscal department, the Wardrobe, during the period of its greatest activity, between the reigns of Henry III. and Henry VII.

The history of the mint is a subject of independent interest and almost equal magnitude with that of the Exchequer itself, while the ministry of the Wardrobe is for the most part connected with constitutional history. It may be noticed, in conclusion, that although the royal treasury continued to be fixed at the five centres previously mentioned down to the present reign, a complete revolution was effected in the procedure of this branch of the Exchequer by the rise of the modern Treasury Board in the seventeenth century. The Treasury, from the Restoration at least, became in common parlance the state department situate, then as now, in Whitehall. Finally, with the foundation of the Bank of England, and the use of Exchequer bills, the last days of the ancient treasury were at hand. Its sole remaining functions, the custody of the regalia and records, have at length been assigned to other departments. The Tower alone, though shorn of its 'lions' and its mint, retains many vestiges of its fiscal guardianship, with a respectable antiquity of something more than six hundred years.

CHAPTER II.

TREASURE AND RECORDS.

THE oft-quoted 'hoard' of the West Saxon kings may be supposed to have contained a very miscellaneous assortment of treasure. Only a century later this was held to include not only coined money or bullion, but also rich vestments, jewels and plate of every description, and even books or records. These, in fact, continued to form the normal contents of the treasury down to our own day, but many other articles of quasi-intrinsic value or imperial interest may be conjectured, and are sometimes enumerated, including relics and money-dies, regalia and rusty armour.

The money-treasure itself was the chief object of attention at the hands of the officials of the Receipt of the Exchequer, in the treasury of which department it will be remembered that the incoming revenue was hoarded. In Saxon, Norman, and early Plantagenet times, we are told, 'money' and 'penny' were interchangeable words, and as the only legal tender at the Exchequer was by weight, a pound of silver pennies was as readily accounted for as any other denomination. At first, indeed, it seems to have been the custom to receive several branches of the revenue ' by tale, namely, by telling over the incoming treasure at the rate of 240 pence to the pound. The revenue in question having been only recently realized by the commutation of a fixed tribute of oxen, sheep, and grain for bullion, the quality of the latter was not at first examined too closely, but the condition was soon imposed that all payments should be tested by the Exchequer scale, sixpence on every pound being exacted to 'trim the balance.' This calculation was, however, found to be unduly favourable to the accountants in an age when clipping and sweating were reduced to fine arts. Moreover, the lowness of the assessments, and the enormous profits gained by enterprising sheriffs, made it only reasonable that the stipulated sums should form a nett revenue, apart from the commercial importance of maintaining a pure currency. Therefore, it was next decreed that all the king's farms should be accounted for by the actual weight of the sum required, a deduction of one shilling in the pound being allowed in most cases as an equivalent.

This official sharp practice was met by the tender of debased coinage, so that another sweeping regulation was enforced in the case of the chief item of the revenue, the royal farms.   By virtue of this innovation, which is ascribed to Roger, Bishop of Salisbury, himself, the farms rendered by the sheriffs were, with few exceptions, subjected to an assay, the treble deficit in number, weight, and purity of the coinage being borne by the accountant.   Besides these silver pennies, all kinds of obsolete or outlandish coins were occasionally received at the Exchequer from distant and uncivilized countries, from foreign merchants or Jewish usurers, and even in the shape of treasure-trove.   These were either used as 'counters,' or converted with other condemned pieces into plate for the service of the king's hall or chapel. Spurious coins were carefully preserved for the sake of example, or as curiosities, and some of these exist in the present day.   It is scarcely necessary to observe that the denominations mark and half-mark, so often met with in old accounts, had no real existence either in gold or silver currency.

For a considerable period after the institution of a specific currency, payments in kind were still accepted at the Receipt of the Exchequer, usually in cases of fines or oblations offered to obtain the king's favour or pardon, or from tenants by serjeanty.   Thus palfreys and hawks were constantly accounted for and consigned to the king's stables and mews respectively. We have rare notices of perfumes, jewels, plate, and furs or vestments being received in the same way, though often directly by the Chamber or Wardrobe treasuries.

The coined treasure, when paid in at the Receipt, was counted, weighed or assayed, as the case might be, and arranged in convenient *rouleaux*, by means of turned boxes or canisters of several sizes, for five pounds or one hundred pounds. These were then deposited in sacks or chests, securely fastened and sealed. The coins selected for the assay, to the value of forty-four shillings, were placed in a particular box, which has given its name to the trial of the *Pyx*.

In addition to money and the apparatus connected with its due receipt and custody, the most valuable portion of the occasional contents of the treasury remains to be noticed, namely, the regalia, crown jewels, and plate. These seem to have been especially costly in early times, both on account of the natural propensity of a rude age to indulge in displays of barbaric riches, and also in conformity with the economic theory of the period, whereby wealth was regarded only as a tangible possession. It is probable, in fact, that a surplus revenue was systematically converted into plate or jewels, in which form it was realized with equal facility, and with a possible appreciation in value due to religious or personal associations and excellence of workmanship. Throughout the Middle Ages, and, indeed, on certain occasions in far later times, the regalia were systematically pawned, at one time with foreign usurers, and at another with the corporation of London, or a more than half-unwilling baron. In the year 1385, with ill-success abroad and disaffection at home, and the spending power of the crown threatened by appropriation of supply, we find in a contemporary record that Richard II. came suddenly to London from Eltham, dined at his Palace of Westminster, and thence proceeded to the royal treasury to view the jewels there. Not long afterwards the king's great crown was pawned to the City of London for £4,000. In fact, the redemption of the regalia, or, at least, their necessary repair and purification, formed an incidental expense of the coronations of most English kings.

The regalia are frequently described in ancient inventories of the treasury, and among other items are mentioned the four crowns—the great crown of King Edward, the second and third crowns and the chaplet—the ampulla, several sceptres—whereof two were called the rod of Moses and the rod of Aaron respectively—spurs, bracelets, and robes of red velvet. At the coronation of Richard I. the regalia were borne in the procession on a chequered table. As early as the reign of

Henry II. we find notices of the swords of state, three in number, which form as it were the link between the regalia proper and the relics deposited in the treasury. These swords were in all probability the legendary weapons, known as the sword of Athelstan, which cleft the rock of Dunbar, the brand of Welland the smith, celebrated in Scandinavian sagas, and the sword of Tristan, which may also be identical with the ' pointless curtana.' Besides these there was the inlaid sword of Edward the Black Prince, the poisoned dagger with which Edward I. was stricken at Acre, and the gauntlet worn by John, King of France, at the battle of Poitiers, with other ancient armour of historic interest.

Amongst the relics proper may be noticed the cross of Gneith (St. Neot's) and the black rood of Scotland. The former of these, as already mentioned, was highly prized by Edward I. A special keeper was assigned to it when it followed the king in his Scotch wars, it being used, like the black rood, for the purpose of administering the oath of fealty to the Scottish barons. It was kept in a separate case, which was broken open by the robbers of the treasury in 1303. Perhaps this was the great jewelled crucifix described by Podelicote in his confession as being among the contents of the three great pouches buried by him near St. Margaret's Church. It may have been mutilated at this time, for we read some years after of a new foot being made for it by the king's goldsmith in the Tower.   There was another cross preserved in the treasury which had once belonged to St. Louis of France, and to the same period belonged the 'golden rose' bestowed upon Edward I. by the pope.   It is well known that a similar honour was conferred upon Henry VIII., together with the present of a two-handed sword inlaid with gold.   A less orthodox relic was the magic sapphire ring supposed to render the wearer invincible in battle.   Many other relics might be enumerated before the Reformation, and even in the reign of Henry VIII. seven valuable crucifixes were still in existence.   Tabernacles were also much in fashion, and from the fifteenth century onwards 'images' of St. George abounded.   Among the more national trophies of the latter half of the Middle Ages may be mentioned the gold sword of Spain and the tablet of Spain, which may have been obtained through the Black Prince or his younger brother, John of Gaunt.   Other historic jewels are spoken of, as the tablet of Burgoigne, the tablet of Bourbon, the tablet of England and France, and the tablet of Lancaster.   All these were of gold, richly ornamented with precious stones.

Although the greater part of the five coffers, filled with relics, which existed in the abbey in

Saxon times, has been lost or dispersed, several of the articles enumerated above may be referred to this period. For instance, the pieces of the true cross and the tunic without seam appear as late as Henry VI.'s reign, being first mentioned in the enrolment of the Confessor's charter of foundation.

A very fair idea of the contents of the mediæval treasury may be found in Podelicote's confession, printed in the preceding chapter. At the close of the Tudor period we are struck with the preponderance of precious stones, elaborately cut and set, over the cumbrous metal-work of an earlier age. Elizabeth in particular was a great collector of precious gems, profiting by her interest in the adventures of the English privateers. Perhaps the most remarkable of the many fine jewels preserved in the Tower in the reign of her successor was the 'Mirror of Great Britain,' a gold jewel set with a very large diamond, a ruby to match, and two other diamonds, one being known as the stone of Scotland. From this time onwards great demands were made upon the jewel-house in connection with the diplomatic service and the private munificence of the sovereign. The auditors' privy seals and jewel office warrants of the seventeenth century furnish information parallel with the ancient inventories of the Plantagenet kings, but rather in the direction of spending than of hoarding. Later still the patronage of the turf made a fresh outlet for the stock of royal plate, but even by the commencement of the seventeenth century, these portions of the king's treasure had ceased to be included amongst the contents of the treasury of the Receipt.

From the earliest times the royal seal appears to have been preserved with the greatest care in the treasury, where it is described in the reign of Henry II. as the inseparable companion of Domesday Book. In the reign of Edward III. several distinct seals are enumerated, and these were then preserved with the regalia. Besides the Great Seal of England, used in the chancery, there was a great seal of the English possessions in France, the seal of the principality of Wales, that of the chancery of Ireland, and, during the vacancy of the see, of the bishopric of Durham. There was also the seal of Calais, which was deposited here in the twenty-ninth year. During the king's frequent absence abroad, his son Lionel, as 'guardian of England,' used a privy seal, which was afterwards cancelled, and a new one struck for Thomas of Woodstock. The two seals in use in the Courts of King's Bench and Common Pleas for the despatch of judicial writs were deposited in the treasury, and the great seal of the Receipt of the Exchequer, mentioned in the *Dialogus*, was in existence here down to the seventeenth century.

All the above seem to have been made of silver. There were many private seals, from that of Lancaster down to a simple knight's; also the leaden or golden seals affixed to papal bulls or diplomatic documents. The great seal was not infrequently counterfeited, and one of these counterfeits was formerly preserved in the treasury.

RECORDS.

It has frequently been remarked that from the earliest times the practice obtained of depositing the national records for safety in the king's treasury. We might even go so far as to suggest that the official preservation of the records takes precedence in certain aspects of the custody of the treasure. Thus the house of the rolls in Babylon contained the treasure of the Assyrian kings, and the temple-treasuries of ancient Greece and Rome were equally dignified as receptacles of records. In Western Europe the same practice prevailed after the Christian era, the king's chapel or some church of royal foundation being the chosen repository of the regalia, jewels and relics, which are rightly described in the most ancient inventories as being 'without price.' The records which bore them company were at least equally priceless in the estimation of their ancient and modern custodians alike. From the lowest point of view these evidences of the king's title to lands, revenues or taxes, records such as Domesday Book, the Exactory Roll, and the Red Book of the Exchequer, were, like the rod of Aaron, and the consecrated oil of the ampulla, part of the stock-in-trade of royalty during the Middle Ages.

It is obviously fitting that the custody of the records should have been confided to that class which alone was skilled in their compilation or use. In this country, however, a dual control existed from very early times, in the best interests of the royal service—on the one hand the house-hold thanes, chamberlains, marshal and constable, with lay underlings, as ushers and serjeants ; and on the other hand the household clerks, chancellor and treasurer, with their clerical staff. But whether clerks or laymen were most in favour at court at particular times, nothing is more striking than the elaborate precautions taken for the safety and accessibility of the records by successive genera-tions of officials.

It was an ancient rule of the treasury of the Exchequer, that no treasure or records could be removed without the authority of the king's writ. In fact the receipt or issue of records were subject to precisely the same conditions as prevailed in the case of money, regalia, plate and jewels, a note being made of their number and description, from whom they were received or to whom issued, and the exact place of their deposit in the treasury, with the respective dates. In spite of this excellent regulation, it was found necessary before long to establish further precautions. The multiplication of legal departments in the reign of Edward I. was followed by a corresponding division of control over the records at large. The barons in their new court had still constant need of many different records for inspection, and these could no longer be simply brought up from the lower Exchequer beneath the same roof. The Wardrobe, which had usurped many of the functions of the treasury, claimed equal access to the rolls of account. The Chancery had formerly been regarded as the clerical department of the Exchequer, and its authority in this matter could scarcely be gainsaid, and finally privy councillors or other ministers of the crown seem to have been constant offenders 'by virtue of their familiarity with the king.' Therefore in the year 1327 a mandate was issued, at the instance of Bishop Stapleton, then treasurer, in accordance with which the entire contents of the record repository were arranged, classified, and numbered, especial pains being taken to affix to each record a distinctive label, so that it might be produced without difficulty and replaced in its proper position.

The records deposited in the royal treasury were preserved in similar receptacles to the bullion, namely, in large chests and smaller coffers, boxes,

4

and hampers.   These chests and coffers were very massive, being bound with iron and secured with three separate locks and keys, according to the usual practice of the period.   One of these chests still survives, being, it is believed, that which used to contain some portion of the regalia together with Domesday Book (see Frontispiece).   This chest is 3 feet 7½ inches in length, 2 feet 3 inches wide, and 2 feet 3 inches deep.   The woodwork is 2 inches in thickness, sheeted with iron within and without, and strengthened by iron bands fastened with iron nails, the heads of which are each more than an inch in breadth.   There are three massive locks, and an inner compartment, probably for the reception of the crown or of the great seal.   This chest, which must weigh at least 5 cwt., was undoubtedly one of the receptacles of the old treasury in the abbey, whence it was removed to the Public Record Office about the year 1857. The locks have been forced open at some remote period, possibly in the robbery of the treasury under Edward I.   It should be added that in the earlier period these chests were frequently conveyed, with their contents, to some distant city or palace.   On these occasions they were described as the arks or hutches of the treasury, the latter term being possibly derived from the frequent practice of including the king's hawks in the treasure-train.   Coined money was also frequently

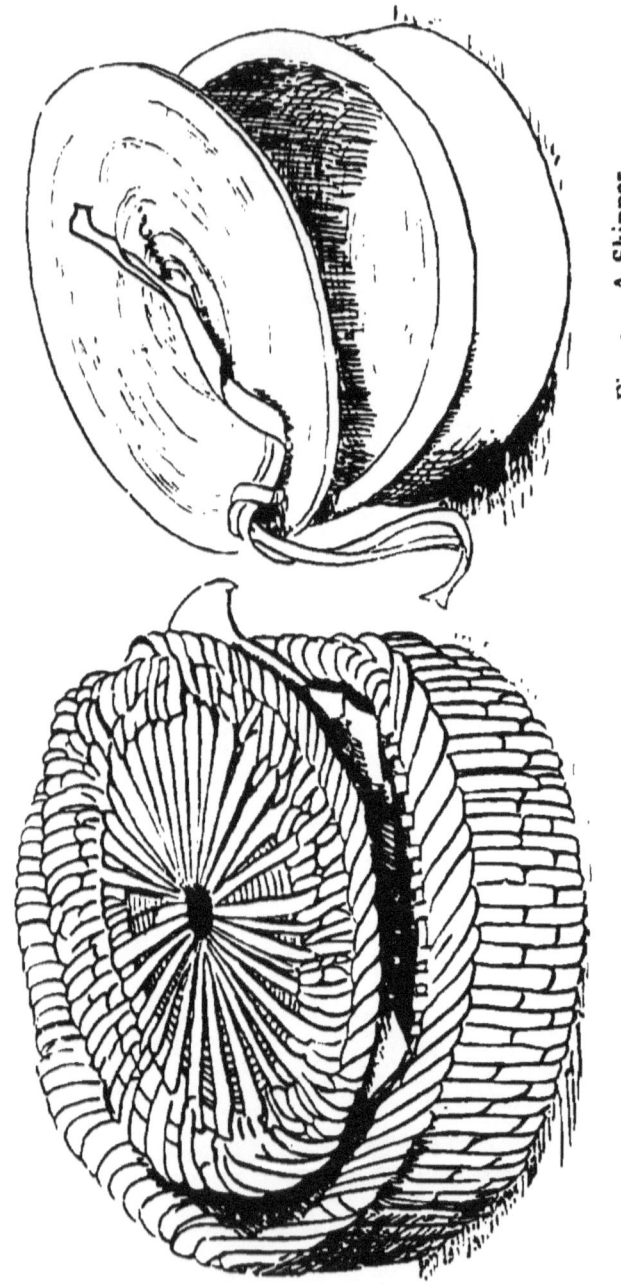

Fig. 3.—A Skipper.

Fig. 2.—A Hamper.

conveyed in wine-casks. The smaller boxes were of wood, often turned in the lathe. There were also hampers in common use, beautifully woven of willow twigs, in somewhat round or beehive shape, together with leather or canvas bags, some of which were curiously painted in oil colours. These bags or pouches, with the turned boxes, or 'skippets,' were placed several together inside a larger case, or 'pyx,' or in a hamper, which in turn was deposited in one of the chests or coffers. The following notice, being one of many hundred similar entries in the memoranda of the treasury, describes the nature of several of these receptacles.

'Be it remembered, that on the 20th day of May, in the 42d year of King Edward the third since the Conquest, there were delivered into the King's Treasury, to be preserved [there], one hamper covered with black leather, and bound with iron, and sealed; and one small bag of canvas with sealed muniments contained within the same; and one pyx with the Treaty of Scotland, made the first day of September, in the 41st year, contained within the same. And they are placed in the lesser chest with three locks above the Receipt, with this device—S.'

In course of time the number of these record-chests was greatly multiplied. In the reign of Henry II. they contained already, besides Domesday Book and the great year-rolls of the Exchequer,

a vast number of charters and other title-deeds;
and these were being constantly added to by
escheats or surrenders in favour of the crown.
More space was fortunately made for their reception by the removal of the Exchequer court a
century later. It is probable that the place of
their deposit, so frequently mentioned as 'above
the Receipt,' refers to the chamber formerly used
for the session of the court, and that the tellers'
chamber, in which records were occasionally
stored, was the inner or council chamber, on the
same floor, usually known from the sixteenth
century onwards as the 'Tellers' loft.' The
adjacent chapel of St. Stephen's was also utilized
for this purpose, but in the course of the next two
centuries this pressure was relieved by the establishment of two new treasuries, one in the gate-
tower of the new palace, and the other in the
chapter-house of the abbey.

It will be gathered from the above entry that a
private mark or cipher was employed to designate
the nature of the contents of the various chests.
This, indeed, was nothing less than a rude form of
symbolism, often extending no further than picture-
writing. Thus, the letter S, in the passage quoted
above, evidently stands for 'Scotland.' Initial
letters were frequently used for this purpose, often
in a hieroglyphic form as monograms. The unequalled collection of papal bulls in the treasury of

the Receipt were arranged by Bishop Stapleton under the letters of the alphabet. In many cases the names or subjects were written in full, but most frequently of all a rude but characteristic drawing was made upon the label, doubtless to assist the operations of unlettered ushers or serjeants. Specimens of some of these symbols are given below. It should be observed that, in addition to the inscription on the label, its exact counterpart was entered in the margin of the inventories of the treasury, of the rolls of the court, and of every other record in which the subject-matter was cited from time to time. Many of them were also more elaborately executed in the several entry books of the Exchequer, such as the Liber A and Liber B.

Fig. 4.—An Acquittance.

Fig. 5.—A Coronation.

Fig. 6.—A Cardinal.

Fig. 7.—Church Reform.

Fig. 8.—The Abbot of Peterborough.

Fig. 9. — A Bishop.

Fig. 10.—A Charter surrendered to the Crown.

Fig. 11.—Oath of Fealty, etc.

Fig. 12.—A Royal Marriage.

Fig. 13.—An Usurer.

Fig. 14.—John, Earl of Holland, Richard II.'s half-brother, and a fashionable Courtier.

Fig. 15.—Alice Perrers, Edward III.'s mistress.

Fig. 16.—Westminster Abbey.

Fig. 17.—The town of Yarmouth.

Fig. 18. — Wales — a Welsh Mercenary.

The records which figured most conspicuously round the Exchequer tables, or which were in daily use in the Barons' chamber, or in the Receipt, comprise several of the most ancient and valuable classes extant.   Besides Domesday Book itself and

the various other compilations intended to discover
the liabilities of the military tenants of the crown,
such as the Red and Black Books of the Exchequer,
the 'Testa de Nevill,' the 'Book of Aids,' and
similar feodaries, there were precise statements of the
royal farms payable by the sheriffs in every county,
namely, the Exactory Roll (now entirely lost to us)
and the assessments drawn up in the fourteenth
century for a like purpose. The treasurer's great
roll (better known to us as the Pipe Roll) and the
chancellor's counterpart formed the ledgers of the
Exchequer, wherein the results of the audit of the
sheriffs' particular accounts were tabulated. Day-
books of receipts and expenditure were also kept
—the Issue and Receipt rolls of the two Remembrancers—which show the exact amounts paid into
the Receipt and issued thence from day to day.
The results of the barons' deliberations in their
council-chamber were recorded in the Memoranda
rolls. The king's writs received at the Exchequer,
or made out there, for money to be paid over and
for other necessary purposes, form a distinct class
of records. Just as nothing of importance could be
transacted without this authority, so nothing could
be undone without a like warrant to stay the
inexorable processes of this court. It was only
after a wearisome contest that the king's writ was
allowed to be presumed in favour of the barons
themselves and others, like the knights of the

Temple and of St. John, who were notoriously exempt from general taxation. These writs were not only imperatively required for every fiscal transaction, but were also closely examined in the course of the half-yearly audits, and therefore were in constant evidence at every stage of the proceedings. A vast number of miscellaneous instruments, such as charters, chirographs, and particulars of accounts, complete the list of official documents most frequently in use for the ceremony of passing the sheriffs' accounts.

In addition to the above characteristic records of the Exchequer, the repositories within the treasuries at Westminster contained many others officially consigned to the treasurer and chamberlains by the Common Law courts, to a certain extent by the Chancery, and quite systematically by those entrusted with the management of the personal expenditure and correspondence of the crown. Of the former class, the custom of depositing fines for conveyance of land for safe custody in the king's treasury is believed to be more ancient than the Conquest, and for several centuries the judges were in the habit of delivering in their rolls and receiving them back whenever needed for temporary reference. Of the latter class, the diplomatic correspondence, including treaties and papal bulls, royal wills and marriages, etc., was in all times very highly prized and jealously guarded. Many of the most ancient of these instruments, some enriched with golden seals, have disappeared long since, but others still survive, such as the 'three golden leagues' of Alphonso the Wise, Francis I., and Pope Clement VII.* These diplomatic instruments may be further considered as the nucleus of our unequalled national collection of state papers, but besides the records of the Curia itself, those of many other departments were deposited here in the ordinary course or from special considerations: the accounts of the army and navy, of the royal household, and of the customs, etc., statutes of Parliament, and others too numerous to mention.

* See pp. 163, 171, 211.

CHAPTER III.

THE EXCHEQUER HOUSE.

ALTHOUGH the Exchequer, as a member of
the king's court, is in some respects the
oldest judicial assembly in the kingdom, there are
good reasons for believing that its functions were
performed in the earliest times following the Conquest by one of its departments alone, the treasury.
Here, then, it will be seen that history has once
more repeated itself, since the latter department
has practically since the Restoration, and definitely
since the reign of William IV., taken the lead in
the financial administration of this country.

It is true that ancient writers, followed by more
recent authorities, have claimed for the Exchequer
an antiquity considerably greater than that which
is usually assigned to it, the reign of Henry I.;
but the scanty evidence that exists points to the
employment of a much more primitive expedient
for auditing the revenue during the reigns of
the first two Norman kings. As the Exchequer

of Normandy was of later date than the similar
institution in England, the tradition of its introduction by the Conqueror will not bear inspection.
Neither is it possible, as some have suggested,
on the authority of certain passages in Domesday
Book, wherein mention is made of fixed farms
rendered to the crown, to connect the Anglo-
Norman Exchequer of the twelfth century with
the financial organization of the eleventh.

Of course Saxon kings possessed crown lands,
and considerable sums were levied at times by the
state, notably the Danegeld, which must have
been accounted for ; but the only trace of a
revenue department before the beginning of the
twelfth century is found, as has been stated, in
connection with the royal treasury. The evidence
in question is clearly unsatisfactory, but it is better
than the confused and purely conjectural account
given of the origin of the court itself by writers
who lived within one generation of the received
date of its establishment. There is only one positive statement which can be depended on, and
this is to the effect that the audit held in the
latter part of the twelfth century at the Exchequer
formerly took place 'at the Tallies.' This expression in itself denotes the actual place of receipt
and issue of the revenue rather than a court or
council chamber.

Our first intimate acquaintance with the position, contents, and machinery of the court of Exchequer is formed through the notices contained in the Pipe Rolls of the reign of Henry II., and the still more detailed description furnished by the author of the *Dialogus de Scaccario* about the year 1177.

But previous to this we have positive knowledge of the establishment of a royal Exchequer early in the reign of Henry I., under the auspices of the great Bishop of Salisbury, Roger le Poer, with whose family its organization is exclusively associated down to the close of the twelfth century. We have seen that during the first half of this century the king's treasury had the Castle of Winchester for its principal centre, and in the same way tradition has assigned the king's Palace of Westminster as the site of the contemporary sessions of the Exchequer. The Exchequer, indeed, is more closely connected with the archæology of Westminster than any other secular institution before the reign of Edward I. It is true that from this date the ancient palace was the fixed seat of the law courts, in which the Exchequer court was thenceforth merged ; but so long as the king's court and Exchequer were distinct, though parallel departments, the latter really monopolized the official establishment at Westminster. It may be urged, however, that in this archæological aspect the king's court is the older institution, held here

possibly in King Edward's day, in the White
Hall or Painted Chamber, and transplanted by
the Red King to a more dignified habitation in the
Great Hall, with which it has ever since been
associated. But it is obvious that this view of
the matter entirely assumes the permanent or
official establishment of the king's court at any one
centre. In truth, it had no such establishment,
but followed the king from one palace to another,
its members being for the most part household
officers as expert as any barons of the Exchequer,
but differing from the latter in this important
particular, that they had no *impedimenta*—in the
shape of a chequered table, a score or so of iron
chests stuffed with rolls and books of reference,
an equal number of bins full of tallies and writs
for every English county, and a smelting furnace
—but could assemble anywhere and decide off-
hand a knotty point of law.

Therefore the Great Hall of Rufus must not
be looked on as the home of the king's court
before the thirteenth century, for it was not necessarily used as a court-house, even when the court
happened to be at Westminster, at the feast of
Pentecost, or for any other purpose than a council,
a coronation feast, or some other imposing ceremony. In any case, however, when the king,
after a few days' stay, had recommenced the
round of his more favoured hunting-lodges, West-

minster knew the court no more until the next
fitful visit of royalty, and absolutely no trace of
its official existence was left behind, except the
records of the court, bundles of rolls, and bales
of writs, which appear to have been deposited in
the treasury of the Receipt of the Exchequer.

Now, it is the existence of the latter as an
essential department of the Exchequer which con-
stitutes the difference between the two great
courts, and explains the existence of a permanent
financial staff under the treasurer and chamberlains
of the Exchequer at Westminster.   The barons of
the Exchequer themselves were scarcely distinguishable, in the time of which we treat, from the
justices of the king's court.   Both were equally
courtiers, and the members of one department were
equally versed in the routine of the other up to a
certain point.   It is only here and there that an
expert stands out as a specialist in jurisprudence
or finance—a Glanvile or a Fitz-Nigel.   These
barons made little longer stay at Westminster than
their brethren of the king's court, though the
period and scope of their work were rigidly
marked out for them ; but at the end of the short
session they left behind them all the apparatus
of their office in charge of deputies, the clerical
staff of the Receipt.   The president and constable
and courtiers of the pattern of Master Brown
went to follow the court, the treasurer and

chamberlains to hover between the king's chamber
and treasury, while the legal barons went on
circuit in the provinces for the nice adjustment
of scutages and assarts. The marshal only was
left with his prisoners and tallies to dispose of.
But in the lower Exchequer, or Receipt, the deputy
chamberlains, the treasurer's clerk, and divers
clerks and serjeants, would be found hard at work
on occasion long after the barons had adjourned.
It is true that during the recess, the majority of
these clerks would return to their normal employment, being paid only for the session, those detained
on the king's business being recognisable by the
extra allowances awarded them, but even so some
regular official must have been in constant residence
at Westminster. Therefore, when the final act of
the session was accomplished—that is to say, when,
after compiling and checking (with much wrang-
ling in their respective master's honour) and sealing
the summonses to the sheriffs against the next
session, the clerks and scribes of the chancellor
and treasurer had returned to the chapel or scriptorium ; when the four tellers had started in charge
of a treasure-train of lumbering carts and great
wooden hutches, that there might be no mysterious
leakage of silver pennies, and the deputy chamberlains had donned armour and mounted horse as
their escort to scare away marauders according to
the terms of their office and the remaining officials

had taken a holiday like their betters, and finally
the marshal, after having seen the usher of the
barons' chamber safely on his way with the
summonses to be served upon the debtors of the
crown in every shire, had himself departed to
change the air of vaults and gaols for the breezes
of the Wiltshire Downs—even then the permanent
establishment of the Exchequer was represented
by the usher of the Receipt, who kept the keys,
and went the rounds of the building night and
morning, while the domestic servants of the absent
usher of the barons' chamber gave heed that there
was no leakage through the tiles upon the chequered
table, and that the moth and rust were excluded
from the hangings of the walls and the linen blinds
of the windows, being overlooked in turn by the
keeper of the king's palace, who was also warder
of the Fleet Prison.

So far the permanent existence of the Exchequer
appears to be established, and these contemporary
indications are confirmed by the unbroken evidence
of its later history since the beginning of the thirteenth century. A difficulty now arises, as we
have seen, in locating this permanent establishment, at Westminster itself in the first instance,
and furthermore at any particular site within the
confines of the royal palace there.

The original position of the Exchequer chamber
seems to have been on the north-east side of

Westminster Palace. There is, indeed, nothing to prove this, except the immemorial tradition of the position of the Receipt in that quarter, the existence of ancient foundations alluded to by Stowe, and the fact of the later transfer of the Exchequer court to the north-west side of the Hall of Rufus after the incorporation of the Exchequer chamber with the common law courts. We may assume, however, that the ' house of the Exchequer' was situated in the river-garden of the old palace. The new palace was admittedly an abortive product of regal ambition, extending no further than the Great Hall ; but before long other buildings of an equally official character were grouped round it, including, in the middle of the twelfth century, a state chapel and the Exchequer house. On the west side of the Hall of Rufus there may have been some temporary buildings, though it is difficult to conjecture their official use, for the constabulary and the more domestic offices of the household dignitaries were probably located in the basement of the old palace. There was one other building within the precincts of the old palace which has a greater interest than any other in connection with the Exchequer. This is the *specula*, or watch-tower, ' near unto the river Thames,' in which the king's treasurer sat when he was ' in residence ' at Westminster in the year 1177. This tower may be with some confidence identified with the Norman structure which formerly abutted on the east side of the Great Hall. It may possibly be further identified with certain 'chambers' which we know were provided for the convenience of the barons in the reign of King John. This tower, communicating directly with the official staff of the king's chapel or Chancery, and also with the king's chamber in the interior of the old palace, and directly overlooking the Receipt with its precious contents. is the real key to the position of the ancient Exchequer. The description of this tower as 'near to the river' may have been necessary to distinguish it from another tower at the southwest angle of the old palace walls, being, indeed, the point furthest removed from the river, and which might be described in contra-distinction to the other as 'near to the church.' The communication between the old and new palaces was apparently by a path from the north-east side of the White Hall. This gave access to the gardens and the river equally, or (by passing through the doors of the chapel) to the watch-tower and Exchequer house, and the south-east side of the new palace yard. But whatever may have been the exact situation of the Exchequer house, we are enabled to form a fairly good idea of its interior plan from the description in the *Dialogus.*

Here we have an upper and a lower Exchequer, both apparently contained in the same building ; for though this appellation may have been merely used to designate their respective importance, we cannot ignore the descriptive sense of those terms where greater and less would otherwise have seemed more appropriate ; and, indeed, we find that the upper Exchequer is called 'the greater' equally with its officers when it was desired to describe its importance rather than its position. There are, however, several other references to Exchequer houses. In the account of the trial of the pyx given in the *Dialogus* we find that the assayer carried the box containing the sample coins selected by him from the heaps undergoing the process of counting and weighing in the Receipt from the lower to the upper Exchequer, and after the coins had been examined, and the pyx sealed by the Barons, he returned, as it would appear, accompanied by the overseers nominated on both sides, once more to the Receipt, where the smelter, 'forewarned' of their approach, had fanned the furnace to the necessary heat. Then as soon as the operation was fairly accomplished, the party returned to the upper chamber to weigh the molten silver in the presence of the Barons. It is just possible, of course, that this operation was really carried out in the treasury of the abbey, where the trial of the pyx was held down to recent times. Each Exchequer was probably divided into two chambers, the upper containing the court-room and council chamber, and the lower a counting-house, also used as a scriptorium, and a treasury. This treasury, however, is described by Elizabethan writers as adjoining the Receipt. There were two ushers or door - keepers, the principal one of whom held a quasi-hereditary office in the upper Exchequer. It was his duty to admit only those who had business to the 'outer chamber,' and none but the Barons to the 'inner chamber.' It is significant that throughout the reign we find this officer paid out of the farm of London. The usher of the Receipt was specially charged with the custody of the treasury door, and he also provided all the necessary implements at a fixed rate, including ink, purchased by him from the sacristan of Westminster. Especial emphasis is laid in the *Dialogus* on the fact that, unlike every other member of the Exchequer, the usher of the upper or Barons' chamber (who was employed at the close of the session in serving the new summonses on the sheriffs) was employed as a permanent domestic servant of the treasurer and chamberlains. This is proof that the Exchequer treasury formed a permanent department at Westminster, and this disposes of the suggestion that after the session the officers of the Exchequer were transferred to

Winchester, together with the contents of the treasury. It was probably also the duty of the senior usher to see that the Barons' chambers were duly swept and aired during the recess, for we read that he was assisted in his duties by the servants of his family. Finally, we have seen that at the beginning of the fourteenth century the barons sent for the two ushers of the Exchequer at Westminster before the recess, and directed them as to special precautions to be taken for the custody of its contents, and this later notice may be fairly considered as explanatory of the earlier practice indicated in the *Dialogus.*

From the end of the thirteenth century onwards, owing to disastrous fires and ambitious schemes of reconstruction, the external position and internal arrangements of the ancient houses were changed beyond all possibility of recognition. The nature of the principal changes that were made in the official economy of the royal Exchequer can, however, be roughly ascertained, and will be found to consist in the complete separation of the Barons' chamber, now dignified with the real, instead of the honorary, appellation of a court, from the lower Exchequer, and its removal to more commodious premises on the opposite side of the Great Hall. The Receipt, however, still retained its ancient site until comparatively recent times, now occupying, apparently, both floors of the

Exchequer house, and administered by an augmented and more dignified official staff, but retaining with the new establishment all the ancient usages and practice of the old.

Although the Exchequer was usually held at Westminster, yet, like the king's court and the treasury itself, it was occasionally located in some other place, though rarely for more than the duration of a single session.   In the stormy reign of King John the Exchequer was twice removed to Northampton, in the 10th and 11th years.   In the 18th year of Edward I. it was ordered to be held at the Husting in the City of London.   In the 26th year of the same reign, and again in the 15th year of Edward II., the Exchequer, including the Receipt and all the treasure, rolls, tallies, etc., was moved bodily to York, owing to the exigencies of the Scotch war.   Here a council chamber or court was specially prepared for the Barons within the castle, the accounts being taken in the great hall of the castle, while the Receipt department found accommodation in the castle tower, which was newly furnished with bolts and bars for the safe keeping of the treasure.   The records were then transferred with every precaution, and under the personal supervision of the sheriffs of the several counties to be traversed.   We read in a contemporary chronicler that they filled twenty-two carts, though the official return only gives eighteen. It is curious to find here already an elaborate division of the Exchequer into official departments, to each of which one or more carts was assigned. The sessions of the Exchequer were so frequently held at York at this time that an alternative scale of allowances or journey money for the sheriffs was prepared according as the Exchequer happened to be in London or at York.

During the whole of the earlier period of its existence the Exchequer was sometimes supplemented by local Exchequers which might or might not be permanent. Such apparently were the Exchequers held at Salisbury, Oxford, Northampton and Winchester. There was an Exchequer for Wales at Carnarvon and Chester, besides those at Carlisle and Berwick, presumably for Scotland, under Edward I.'s protectorship, while the Exchequer at Dublin was very perfectly elaborated. The Exchequer of the Jews formed a parallel department to the central court, and there was also an Exchequer in the Tower in connection with the mint, and another, doubtless, in the Wardrobe. There seems to have been a private Exchequer at one, at least, of the king's hunting palaces, Woodstock. The great Bishop of Winchester had an Exchequer of his own at Wolverley, with machinery capable of producing miniature Pipe Rolls of bailiffs' accounts, and this Exchequer was utilized by the crown during the vacancy of the see.

The last removal of the Exchequer for reasons of state took place in the year 1643, when it was established at Oxford together with a royalist Parliament. It was, however, revived at Westminster in 1654 by the lord protector, and quickly adapted itself to the new methods of finance which arose from the ruins of the old feudal revenue of the crown.

In September, 1666, the Exchequer was once more removed, this time only as far as Nonsuch, 'in the time of y[e] late dreadful fire in London.' The removal, which was by water, occupied several days. Seven barges were pressed for the purpose by the troops who were employed in guarding the treasure and records, which lay scattered in process of packing from Monday to Friday. At the same time the goods and furniture of the several resident officers were also removed.

CHAPTER IV.

THE OFFICERS OF THE EXCHEQUER.

THE clerical establishment of the Exchequer as it existed in the latter part of the twelfth century will be found to have undergone very few changes during the seven hundred years which elapsed since its first institution. Just as there were two distinct departments of the Exchequer house— the upper and the lower—so each had its appropriate staff of officers. In the case of the lower Exchequer, however, it was laid down, as early as the twelfth century, that here the barons or clerks of the upper house were directly represented by their respective deputies or subordinates, and the correctness of this assertion may to some extent be realized by the following classification of the offices in existence during the reign of Henry II.:

Upper Exchequer.	Lower Exchequer.
President.	
Treasurer.	
*Treasurer's scribe.	} Treasurer's clerk.
*Clerk of the rolls.	

Upper Exchequer.	Lower Exchequer.
Chancellor Chancellor's clerk. *Chancellor's scribe.	
Constable. Marshal. *Constable's clerk.	
	Deputy chamberlains. Usher. Tellers.
Chamberlains. *Cutter of the tallies. *Knight assayer. *Melter.	Weigher. Watchman. Clerks, Serjeants, Porters, Messengers.

Of the above officials, the president was normally the justiciar, who represented the sovereign in this as in other capacities. He had the exercise of patronage from the appointment of an usher to the farm of a manor, held Exchequer pleas, and supervised the issue of writs of allowance, etc., to accountants on behalf of the crown.

The chancellor represented the equitable power of the Curia in the Exchequer. There he was the nominal custodian of the great seal, and he checked the accuracy of the treasurer's records in the composition of his own rescripts. At his disposal was a scribe, who copied the great roll, word for word, from the treasurer's clerk, to form the antigraph known as the chancellor's roll. Together with this scribe, the chancellor owned a clerk, whose chief duty it was to overlook his brother of the pen to ensure additional accuracy, for such was the authority of the great roll that its *dictum* would have been maintained in spite of manifest right and equity, were it not possible to check its accuracy by means of this careful rescript. Then, if the chancellor challenged the authority of the leading record, the question at issue was argued before the Barons and decided by them.

The constable was actively employed, with the assistance of his clerk, in paying stipends out of the Receipt of the Exchequer to royal officers and other claimants, after duly investigating their claims. He was also called upon to attest writs with the justiciar.

The marshal's duty was to keep the writs and the returned tallies of the sheriffs' creditors in bundles for each county, to take charge of offenders committed to his custody for contempt of the court, and to take the accountants' oaths. It was also his privilege to pay the salaries and allowances of Exchequer officials; but as these latter were experts, and the coinage of the period none of the finest, it was found necessary to ordain that, if any official noticed a wrong amount or indifferent coinage in the payment made to him (on the spot) he might seek redress, but once beyond the door none of his money was ever exchanged.

The tallies proper were made by a regular

'cutter,' the chamberlain's serjeant. It will be seen in the next chapter that the system was identical with that of the Exchequer table and the Exchequer dots, holding the middle place in point of financial development between the two, between picture-writing, that is, on the one hand, and shorthand on the other.

The chamberlains were two highly-dignified officials, who assisted the treasurer in his arduous labours and shared the responsibilities of his office.

The clerk of the rolls provided suitable scribes, and superintended their labours in the scriptorium.

The office of the treasurer was the most important of any. He had the superintendence of every department, but his especial care was in the matter and composition of the great roll. This was written by his clerk on sheep-skins specially selected. Each single roll was usually composed of two large membranes, and had lines ruled on it from top to bottom. The headings and entries were made at regular intervals, and according to established form and order. In case of a clerical error, no erasure was ever permitted, but an interlineation was made when necessary, to which regulation the use of sheep-skins is attributable, these being most sensitive to erasure.

Besides these important officials, there were two other fiscal experts nominated by the justiciar or treasurer—the master of assays and the assayer —whose duties will be explained in another place.

The four tellers, though here in a subordinate position, became officers of considerable dignity in Tudor and Stuart times, when, in fact, their duties were performed by deputies.

The deputy chamberlains were the most characteristic officers of the Receipt, where, with the treasurer's clerk, they superintended the entire operations connected with the housing of the treasure and records and, under the direction of the treasurer and chamberlains, of the payment of money-orders.

The office of usher was in reality a place of considerable importance and profit. It was granted by Henry II., early in his reign, to Roger of Wallingford, or Roger of the Exchequer, in whose family it was long continued. This office was held by serjeantry, and several of the duties belonging to it were performed by deputies.

There were numerous clerks or serjeants of the Receipt who were employed both in manual operations, such as packing and carting the treasure, and also as messengers.

It is to be observed, however, that those officers marked with an asterisk in the above list were properly members of the Receipt, or of the department known as the scriptorium. These, then, by a military figure of speech, were designated as

6

the 'soldiers' of the superior officers, just as 'pawns' were employed in the chess-game itself. Most of these offices, indeed, were held in fee, or by the performance of some serjeanty, in the same way that so many household offices were held during the Middle Ages. Thus the famous Countess of Albemarle, Isabella de Fortibus, was a chamberlain of the Exchequer, and appointed her own seneschal, Adam de Stratton, as her deputy. It was difficult in any case for the great officers of state to give a regular attendance at the Exchequer, on account of their necessary attendance on the king's person. Thus, in course of time, the chancellor, chamberlains, constable, and marshal ceased to attend, and new clerical officers performed their duties. The office of justiciar was extinct before the reign of Edward I., and the practical administration of the revenue fell into the hands of the treasurer and barons.

Between the reign of Henry II. and that of Edward II. the establishment and constitution of the Exchequer were permanently settled, several important administrative changes being rendered necessary by the continued non-residence of certain officers of the upper chamber. The close connection which existed, in the days of Richard Fitz-Nigel, between the clerks of the king's chapel and the scriptorium of the Receipt, had come to an end with the erection of a chancery department

at the close of the twelfth century. The chancellor, with his vigilant clerk and skilful scribe,
being now employed in other business of state, it
was necessary that their places should be filled by
other officers in order to continue the control of
the treasurer's department, which the crown had
from the first so jealously exercised. From this
time onward, therefore, the duties hitherto performed by the chancellor's staff and special commissioners, like Richard of Ilchester and Master
Thomas Brown, were assigned to a new sub-
division of the Exchequer itself. In appearance
the change was only in name. The comptroller
of the Pipe was the new title of the old scribe of
the chancery, while the chancellor's clerk became
dignified with the familiar title of chancellor of
the Exchequer, just as new offices had formerly
been created for the deputies of the king's constable, marshal, and chamberlains. A little later
still another officer, called the clerk of the writs,
was added to the ex-chancery staff. At the same
time the treasurer himself, being now more
seriously engaged with state affairs, delegated a
large part of his personal duties to his own clerk
and scribe, who were henceforth better known as
the under-treasurer of the Exchequer and the clerk
of the Pipe respectively. The real significance of
these official changes lies in the fact that the whole
staff was for the first time united under the direct

control of the treasurer, the audit of the revenue being checked in the department itself by a simple process of account.

Other material changes in the establishment of the Exchequer were due to the great expansion of its duties at the beginning of the fourteenth century. In the reign of Henry II. it had been the custom for the barons to reserve certain points of daily practice for consideration until the close of the audit, which *memoranda*, as they were termed, were entered upon a separate roll. In course of time these legal notes were considerably augmented through the rapid expansion of the revenue and the increased difficulty of collecting it. To facilitate this work a new officer was appointed in the reign of Henry III., called the Remembrancer. This officer kept the Memoranda Roll, issued processes for the recovery of the king's debts, and acted, in fact, as the solicitor to the treasury. As was usual at this time, the office was executed by two separate clerks, each of whom checked the other, and who were styled respectively the lord treasurer's and the king's Remembrancers. There had also been in use, from the reign of Henry II., a systematic registration of every sum of money received at the Receipt in the roll kept by the treasurer's clerk. It is probable that a similar record was preserved of the sums disbursed there. In any case the two rolls, called respectively the receipt roll and the issue roll, were made up daily, for each term, from the reign of Henry III., the officer in charge of them being thenceforth styled the clerk of the pells. This was the origin of the Pells Office of the Exchequer. The customary check upon the proceedings of the clerk of the pells was furnished by the appointment of a new officer, the auditor of the Receipt, who recorded in duplicate the several receipts and issues.

It was already found difficult at the end of the twefth century to include the entire statement of account prepared by the treasurer every Michaelmas within the compass of the Pipe Roll, and it was not long before a change of practice was made in the preparation of the annual rolls, which gave rise to several new offices. These were the auditors of foreign accounts (every source of revenue not included in the Pipe Roll being called 'foreign'), the clerk of the Estreats, the foreign apposer, and the clerk of the Nichils, the nature of whose employment will be described in another place.

The following notice of the establishment of the Exchequer in the fifteenth year of Edward II. is interesting, not only on account of its probably unique character, but also for the mention it contains of the germ of certain offices which were not previously known to have existed at this date. The occasion of the return was the removal of

the Exchequer from Westminster to York before
alluded to, when the barons who had met to
arrange the details of the removal assigned the
provision of carts made for this purpose in the
following proportions :

The office of Adam de Lymbergh, king's Remem-
    brancer   -   -   -   -   -   2 carts.
The office of William de Fulburne, treasurer's
    Remembrancer   -   -   -   -   3 carts.
The office of William de Everdon and R[obert] de
    Wottone   -   -   -   -   -   2 carts.
The office of John de Catfelde   -   -   -   1 cart.
The office of W. de Bereford, justice of the bench -   2 carts.
The office of Adam de Herewyngtone   -   -   3 carts.
The office of the chamberlains of the Receipt   -   2 carts.
The same for the counter-tallies   -   -   -   2 carts.

Now, although only two Remembrancers are
known to have existed at this date, it is a curious
fact that both William de Everdon and Robert de
Wotton were admitted and acting as such, though
apparently in a subordinate position, and it is probable that we see here the germ of the later office
of secondary of the Remembrancers.   John de Catfelde probably represented the Pells or Auditors
departments; William de Bereford was evidently
responsible for the Records of the King's Bench
and Common Pleas ; Adam de Herewyngtone was
deputy chamberlain, and doubtless had charge of
the furniture of the office, or perhaps of the
treasure-chests ; while the remaining contents of

the Receipt, including the marshal's tallies, were included in the last two entries.

This, indeed, was the age of reorganization at the Exchequer, as we know from the several statutes and ordinances which were framed, doubtless at the instance of energetic treasurers like Bishop Stapleton. But although the Exchequer attained its highest perfection as a court of revenue long before the close of the Middle Ages, its establishment did not reach its greatest dimensions until the close of the reign of Queen Elizabeth, as may be readily gathered from the following instructive table of offices and fees in the year 1593:

Lord High Treasurer, £368, and his robes.

Chancellor of the Exchequer, £113 6s. 8d., and his livery.

Lord Chief Baron, £100, and £20 as justice of assize, and his livery.

Barons, £40 13s. 4d., and livery.

Queen's Remembrancer, £55 14s. 4d., and livery.

Lord Treasurer's Remembrancer, £64 2s. 1d., and livery.

Clerk of the Pipe, £65 4s. 2d.

Comptroller of the Pipe, £15 2s.

Five Auditors (each), £10.

Foreign Apposer, £16 13s. 4d.

Clerk of Estreats, £15.

Clerk of the Pleas, £5.

Two Marshals (each), £2 10s.

Clerk of the summonses, £4.

Two Deputy Chamberlains (each), £5.

Two secondaries of the Queen's Remembrancer, £4.

Three secondaries of the Pipe, £15.

Pipe office clerk for offering amercements, £9 13s. 4d.

Queen's Remembrancer's clerk for writing fines and amercements to crown, £7 13s. 4d.

Lord Treasurer's Remembrancer's clerk for affeering amercements, £22 10s.

Clerk of the Pleas, £61.

Ushers of the court, £140.

Eight porters (each), £4, and livery.

Two chamberlains (each), £52 3s. 4d., and livery.

Under-treasurer of England, £173, and livery.

Clerk of the tallies, £41 13s. 4d., and livery.

Clerk of the Pells, £61 16s. 8d.

Four Tellers (each), £31 13s.

Two joiners of tallies (each), £10.

Clerk to write tallies of comptrolment, £9.

Porter of bags and treasurer's keys, £6 6s. 8d.

Four messengers (each), 4½d. per diem.

Writers of the declaration of revenues of court, £30.

Grooms of the Receipt, £2, and allowance for parchment.

Ushers of Receipt for all extras, paper, wax, etc., £206.

Nearly a century later the composition of the Exchequer staff is found to be almost exactly the same. It appears, however, by a return of the state of the civil list in 1679 that the salaries of all the officers had been largely augmented. On the other hand, they were considerably in arrears, though to a less extent than those of most other public offices—that is to say, only some two years all round instead of eighteen years. The later establishments, from Anne to George III., exhibit few changes, though from the latter reign, of course, the suppression of the more ancient and useless offices proceeded very fast. The chamberlains were abolished in 1782, and in 1784 the appointment of commissioners for auditing the public accounts paved the way for greater changes. Finally, in 1833, the account side, or the Barons' chamber, was swept away, and the lower house, or Receipt, shared the same fate. The office of Queen's Remembrancer alone survived, with the exception of the now obsolete functions of the chancellor of the Exchequer as a baron of the court. The practical work of the Exchequer was henceforth performed by the modern departments of the Paymaster-general and Treasury itself, whilst the place of the Receipt was more commodiously occupied by the Bank of England.

From very early times the officers of the Exchequer had enjoyed complete immunity from ordinary taxation and other liabilities of the subject, and this privilege was guarded by them with great jealousy and remarkable success. Thus in all returns for scutage, Danegeld, or other general assessments, they were specially excepted by name, and these exceptions form a principal means of identifying the members of the court. As late as the year 1690 a special representation was made by the lords of the treasury for the exemption of Exchequer officials from service in the militia on the ground of their immemorial privilege. This was based on the ancient liberties and customs of the court, whereby its members could not be called away to answer any civil action while they were engaged in the king's service. The great precedent book of the Exchequer is full of cases in point carefully entered by the officials for their own protection. These privileges gave great offence to less favoured servants of the crown. The author of the *Dialogus* relates an anecdote of a scene which took place at the Exchequer under Henry II., when the barons were in danger of losing their immunity from taxation owing to the representations made to the king by certain jealous courtiers. Contemporary satirists were also fond of drawing attention to the pedantry and exclusiveness of the official staff, who neglected the service of the altar, to which they were professed, for the rites of the Exchequer table, and who were better versed in the mysteries of the Great Roll than in the teaching of the Scriptures. There is certainly a spirit of professional pride, and a callousness to the sufferings and wrongs of an overtaxed people, observable in the financial administration during the Middle Ages, together with a strong suspicion of personal corruption, and the popular feeling expressed on this subject by the early satirists found some justification in the scandals, punished from time to time by the crown or Parliament, to say nothing of the terrible outbreaks of popular indignation connected with the names of Wat Tyler and Jack Cade.

The official life and surroundings of an officer of the king's Exchequer during the Middle Ages differed little from that of any other trusted courtier or learned priest, or skilful scribe in a country which has been well described by a great historian as a 'paradise of clerks.' The early training in schools and scriptorium was the same, for all alike a dreary curriculum. The practice in the Exchequer and the course of promotion were equally unvarying. Literature was a real solace to some few, while others rose or fell in the slippery ways of politics. The typical official, however, like Alexander de Swereford, the arch-deacon, and Bishop Stapleton, had no thought or interest outside their allotted or self-appointed tasks. During the sessions and terms of the Exchequer they devoted their whole attention to the financial interests of the crown. In their leisure hours they arranged the records of the court, or compiled monumental works of official reference. They lived and died in harness, and their autobio-graphy may be found in a crabbed official hana covering the surface of a thousand parchment rolls, the record of a life's work at the Exchequer.

With the beginning of a new era of personal monarchy and social interest the officers of the Exchequer appear in a more humane aspect. Men like the two Fanshawes were at once skilful officials and shrewd men of the world, the personal friends of statesmen like Winchester, Mildmay, and Cecil. Their official correspondence is infinitely varied, and admits us behind the scenes of many an episode of Elizabethan statecraft. The semi-official correspondence is even more interesting, illustrating the relations which existed between Elizabethan ministers and 'permanent heads' of departments. If Burleigh's coal-merchant is arrested for debt in the act of delivering his lordship's winter supply of fuel, Mr. Fanshawe is requested to settle the matter by an official stroke of the pen. If another honest tradesmen has been informed against for unwittingly breaking the statute by wearing a silk nightcap, he is sent, cap and all, to the obliging Remembrancer, with his lordship's private request that he will 'end the matter with the Customers and let him go.'

The private correspondence is the most valuable of all for our present purpose, and throws a strong light upon the domestic life of a Tudor official. Two letters have been selected for this purpose. The first is one of many similar epistles, written by the wife of one of Fanshawe's colleagues to her husband during his absence from his country-seat on the business of the Exchequer. The other is apparently written by the mother-in-law of a famous Exchequer lawyer.

MR. GAMAGE,

After my verie hartie commendations unto you, you shall understand that I haue sent in the basket a copple of henes, a chesse, a dussen of puddinges, fortie egges, and some apples to fill upp the basket. Also there are iiij puddinges for Edmond Wright out of the bagge. Goodman Birche hathe appointed wth one to paye you certayne money at London ; whether you haue receavid it or not I know not. The small hogges that Hewet had are come home little or nothinge the better for their goinge. If Balstons prove no better, we shall haue no porkers, except we feed them with beanes. Bigge Fridaye's wif hathe caused the corne to be thresshed out which was distrayned for the debte due to Harrise, and Harise prayeth you if you may speake with Mr. Cirsten to geve him knowledge thereof and see what remedie there may be had against them that thresshed it. I thank you for your orrenges wch you sent me, but they were verie muche brused. Thus wth my hartie commendations to my brother and sister I leaue to troble you at this present.

From Kingsey this second of February.

> Your lovinge wif
> DOROTHE GAMAGE.

MY BEASSE,

I prethe commend my kind love to Kitt, and tell him y^t I am nowe at Hartingfordburye soe I cannot speake wth my aunt tell Saterdaye consarninge ye cloke: but if he have a desier to make it up before ye time he maye do it for I am suer she will sell it and I thinke her prise will be reasonable and especially to his frind. Y^e next time Hale cometh after I have spoken wth her he shall knowe ye prise. I have sent the a letle provision agen this time, but I cold wish it were much beter. Ther is a goose pye, a netes tounge pye, and a mutton pastie for standers for thy table this Crismas, for a nede, I knowe they will last tell twelftide for they ar now newe baked. I have sent the a goose and ij capens alive for feare they wold not last tell ye holy daies if they had bin killed, but I wish the to kill them on Saterday at ye furdest lest they growe worse. I hope they ar fatt nowe therfore it were pitye they should fall. Ther is ij cheses, such as I have, and a pott of buter to make thy pyecrust because thou shalt spare thy firkin still tell Lent. If thou be wise perswade Kitt to make no more doings then neds must this Cristmas because of sparinge of his purse for ye first daye of ye terme. I prethe doe soe much as bestoe for me vj^d or viij^d in sume oringes or lemons or ij poun siterns and sende them downe nowe by Hale. I wold have them to give to my La : Pernerton wth sum other things (capens) for a New-yers Guift. I mene to give it nowe before I ge backe. I have nowe sent the my best fine sheete because thou hadst a mind to it for thy Newyers Guift I wold I wer able to give the and Kitt as

good a Newyers Guift as I cold wish but as thou
lovest me send me none but this that I desier the,
a pair of cut fingred strong longe gloves, not
white, to wer every day, of viij^d; and I prethe send
me a mask for my selfe for I was dreven to send
away my setten on to Nan Darnall for a token and
my other is verye bad ; and so wth my best wishes
to thee & Kitt I rest

Thy Mother   S. D.

I prethe good Bes have a good sisterly care over
Mall for nowe she is in ye makeng or marring.
Make her goe clenly & nete in her clothes, and
call on her for reding and writing, and locke what
nesaries she doeth want let her have them : when
I com I will recken wth the for all.   I prethe let
her goe abrod wth the whene it is fitt she may goe
y^t she may lerne howe to behave her selfe by seing
of others.   And so agen far well   Comend me to
my pretye boyes and give them ther aple pastis
from me.   I am sorrye I have no beter thing to
send my prety knaves.   I pray God in Heaven
blesse them and all our postrity. Amen.   Ther is
for every on a pasty, on for the.   I have sent up
thy fether for she if thou thinkest good, if hats be
in fashon, or els twill do her no good.

I have sent the a rabet for thy super for it will
not last, thou sholdes have had a cople if I cold
got them.

I protest to thee I have not had an egge ilaied of my owne hens since thou wentest to London; nor I thinke shall not till Shrovtide, nor we can scerse get any here or els I wold send L mor then I doe.

Y^e capens fed themselves, they were not cramed.

[Endorsed]   To M^{RIS} VERNON.
This be
d.d.

It would appear from the above and many similar letters of the period that the new school of clerks were more occupied in the pursuit of private wealth than in the scientific investigations of their mediæval predecessors.   There were, of course, others whose duties necessitated a permanent residence at Westminster, and whose everyday life is faithfully described in the curious and unique document which is printed below.

RIGHT HONOURABLE AND MY SINGLER GOOD M^R
My humble duetie withe weepinge teares remembred.   It may please yor honoure to understande that on Frydaye beinge the xxth of this presente Marche all the tellers and other officers of the Receipt were in their severall offices, where they contynewed till xj of the clokke of the same daye, at whiche tyme they breake uppe, leavinge their

offices in safetie (as they have ben accustomed) to
my custodie and chardge; so departinge they went
their waies: after whose departure I shut the dores,
barringe and lockinge the same and brought the
kaies therof into my kitchen, where I hanged the
same upon an yron hooke appoyncted *&* dryven
into one ende of the mantel-tree of the same
kitchen chymeney. In the whiche kitchen I with
my wief and famylie have used to make our most
abode bothe at worke dyner and supper. And at
night afore wee goe to our beddes I with some of
the rest of my servauntes haue used to take the
same kayes and to open the dores of the same
Receipt to viewe the same under the bordes *&*
all other corners, whiche doone I haue likewise
used to locke the same and so to bringe the kaies
therof into my bed chamber where also uppon a
like nayle or hooke I hange the same untill the
next morninge. This notwithstanding my right
honourable *&* singuler good Mr. I consideringe
this myssehappe and most unfortunate chaunce to
come onlye throughe myne owne faulte and more
then beastly neglygence in so lewdelye abusinge
my self, neyther wayeinge myne allegeaunce whiche
I owe to my moste gratiouse soveraigne the
queenes royall ma^tie, neither ponderinge myne othe
whiche I tooke at my first cominge to the same,
neyther yet consideringe the greate credite comytted
unto me of so great a make of tresere, of all others

moste unworthy the same, all whiche considerations
(right honourable) dryve me to bewaile my
wretched fortune and happe to come from God
onelie most justelye for my neglygent servinge of
God, whiche is the utter undoinge of me my poure
wief, child & famylie for ever.   For the whiche
I am moste hartelie sorry euen from the verie
bottom of my wretched & myserable hart
(Almightie God is bothe witnes and judge of the
same, bedewed withe salte & wepinge teares
daye & night).   But alas this sore can nowe in
no waies bee salved, consideringe my poure estate
and lacke, but onlye by the queenes highnes most
mercifull pardone and forgyveness of the same.
In liewe whereof I confesse myself to deserve her
highnes most grevous and hevie displeasure.   The
remembrance therof considered dothe and shall
greeve me dueringe my lief.   And furder waigh-
inge the haynous offence by me commytted against
my verye good lord, my lord threasurer, whome
God longe preserve, whose great goodness both I
and myne have often felte to our great comforte.
Moreover the consideracon whiche I nowe see and
fele in abusinge the great goodnes of yor honoure
extended towardes me dyverse tymes in callinge
upon mee to looke warelie and carefullie to my
chardge, office and servauntes, all whiche considerations advertisementes and good wareninges
mought have sufficed enoughe and to to well, if I

myserable wretche had not been to to forgetfull, lewde and neglygent. And lastelie when I consider that I stande bounde unto Sr Percivall Harte, Knight, gentleman Hussher of the Receipt and Starchamber in the some of 500£ to save him harmeles ageinst the queenes highnes for his said offices (unles I maye taste the compassion of my said good lord threasurer's helpe and your honours) I certeynely know and shall assuredly feele the utter destruction of mee and myne in this world for euer. But alas why doe I thus longe trouble your honoure whereas I ought rather go too the matter, namelie where how and when I withe my evell servauntes haue bestowed our selfes; from Friday firste mentioned untill the Mondaye then next following, at whiche tyme about ix of the clocke the same mysfortune was first espied.

For true declaration wherof it may please your honour to understand that the same Frydaye in the afternoone I withe other the hed boroughes of Westminster did attend on Mr Hodgeson for the survey of the commen sewer of Westminster by comandement of my said good L. Treasurer. In the same present tyme I sent Wm Marshall to Mr Taillo^r withe a byll obligary for x^{ll} to be repayed at the feast of Pentycost next, whiche money the same Marshall brought me about vj of the clocke at night. And for bycause my other ij servauntes

were appoyncted to receyve the holly comunyon
on the morrowe, being Satterday and Easter even,
withe my ij mayd servauntes, I commaunded theym
to prepare theym selfes, their clothes and necessaries for the worthy and decent receyving of the
same ; so that during that tyme I requered of
theym no manyer attendaunce nor service. The
next day being Satterdaye they and my said mayd
servauntes did receyve the same holly communyon,
whiche done they came home and dyned wᵗ me at
myne owne table, and after dynner walked abrode
till evening prayer tyme where they abode in the
churche dureing the same, which finisshed they
went into Westminster Hall and there played
secretlye by the space of one houre or thereabout,
I and my wief standinge by and beholding the
same. And then the night approaching I comanded theym to leave of their playe and to shutt
and barre and locke the dores of the Receipt: and
broughte the kaies into my chamber and hanged
theym upon the nayle dryven into a post fast by
my beddeside, where they remayned till the morrowe being Easter daye and about vij of the
clocke Willᵐ Marshall tooke the same bunches of
kayes sayeing, 'Sir, I will looke into the Receipt
to se if all thinges bee well,' and retorning brought
the same kayes and placed theym as before uppon
the same post, sayeing 'All is well.' That same
daie I and my wief receyved the same holly com-

munion; my said servauntes attending on us brought
us to the paroche church where duering dyvine
service I thinke they remayned also, for at our
departure from the said churche about x of the
clokke we came home where I leaving my wief
and mayd servauntes I and my men servauntes
went ageyn to the Colledge and parisshe churche
where also we contynewed till xj of the clokke.
At which houre we tooke our dynner accompanyed
with iij or iiij^{or} poure old women, the whiche
receyved the same day also. In the afternoone of
the same daye, ymediatly after dynner, I with my
wief and my mother, my doughter and Edmund
Gilbert, went into St Georges Field by the bote of
one Roger of Wastminster, waterman, and return-
inge backe went to the Churche to eveninge
prayer; whiche fynished I with other hed boroughes
went into the vestrie to heare and ende a matter in
travers between the wiefes of Wattes and Wheatley
complaynauntes, and the wief of Darloe defendaunt,
whiche wee could not ende at that tyme. And
from thence I went home to supper and so by
daye lyght to our beddes. The next morning
being Easter Mondaye, about vj of the clok I sent
my servaunt Marshall to Mr Hodgson for the
same survey according to his owne appoynetement
made the Satterday before, whiche survey at his
first comyng was not done; whiche fynisshed he
brought unto me in the churche, and being perused

over wee founde the mystakinge of one some, wheruppon it was agreed that Mr John Dodington & I should in the afternoone of the same daye meete together at his house for the new wryting of the same warrant and survey. All this afternoone Marshall attended upon me. And being appoyncted the next morninge to send ageyne for the same survey, being Tuysdaye, about vj or vij of the clok in the morning I sent William Marshall ageyn, appoincteinge him to mete Mr Baylief of Westminster, Mr Dodd and my self at the iij Cranes in the Vintrie. In the meane tyme we lerned that my lord threasurer and my lord of Leicester should dyne at Mr Clarencieulx, wher in the said after noone we wayted on his lordship from whome wee receyved order to bring the Surveiour unto his lordshippe, during which forenone Edmond and William wayted on mee, but in the after noone Wm Marshall wayted on me alone and Edmund and Gilbert remaynted at my house at the Receipt. The same Tuisdaye, at night, William Marshall desired leave of me to lye that night at his owne house in Longdiche. The next morning being Wensdaye the same William cam about vij of the clock into my bedchamber sayeing, Sir I will goe see if all things be in safetie and well in the Receipt, taking the ij bonches of Kaies withe him. And, as he sayed, founde all thinges well ; wheruppon he retorninge withe the same

Kaies hanged theym uppon the same nayle nighe my said bedside. In the meane while I comanded him to dresse and bring myne apparell that I mought rise and go to the churche being our Lady daye, whiche thing he did accordingly; duering whiche tyme my other men servauntes made theym redye to wayte on me to the churche, about viij of the clokke, where I remayned sitting withe Mr Billesby till about ix or neare x of the clokk, at whiche tyme Mr Hogeson came and requested the openyning of the Receipt dores, whiche were opened unto him, sayeing to William 'Have you not a bolt to this dore' who answered, 'No.' 'Give me then ye kayes and I and my man Piers wilbe occupied her this houre.' But as sone as he came to the toppe of the Tellinge Lofte he spied duste in Mr Freakes office, and going a litle furder towardes his owne office, spiede his owne chiste to be spoyld and broken and a great hole over Mr Freakes office, whiche so amased him that he came runnyng downe the Tellinge loft stares and sent his man to the churche for me in all the haste; and sent also for Mr Petre, untell whose comyng he wold not approche nere his said cheste. Thys if it may please yor honour is the whole some of my knowlege towching this my mysfortune to the utter undoinge for ever bothe of me and all myne if my good lord Treasurer and yor honour have not pitie on me whiche I desire for

Christe Jesus sake who long preserve yor honoures in good healthe wth the encrease of muche honour. Written in the Marshalsie, this xxix of Marche 1573

> By yor most humble wretched
> Servaunte
> W. STANTON.

[To S^r Wa. Mildmaye.]

The following report of the ceremony of the installation of the lord high treasurer throws much light on the internal economy of the Exchequer in the reign of Queen Anne.   It is printed here from the Black Book of the Exchequer :

' Monday, the 11th day of May, 1702, the Right Hon. Sydney Lord Godolfin having had the staff of Lord Treasurer delivered to him by Queen Anne, on Sunday the 10th instant, on the 11th he came, about the hour of 10 in the morning, to the house of Lord Halifax, the Auditor of the Receipt of the Exchequer, where he was attended with many Earls, Barons, Privy Councillors, the King's Attorney and Solicitor, and other persons of quality ; they being assembled in the two great rooms were treated with chocolate, etc., by the said Lord Halifax.   The proceedings began from thence ; a great number of gentlemen in swords and coats, pell mell, the Clerks of the Treasury, Auditors of the Exchequer, Secretaries, Officers, etc., and amongst them the officers of the Exchequer, having no gowns (who should have marched in their proper places if they had gowns) ; then the Usher of the Exchequer in his gown, the Clerk of the Pells, Clerk and Tally-writers' Clerk in gowns, the Tally-cutter, the Deputy Clerk of the Pells, the two Deputy Chamberlains, the Marshall of the Exchequer, the Auditors, viz., the Lord Halifax on the right hand of Mr. Lownds, the Secretary to the Lord Treasurer, the Lord Treasurer's Sargeant-at-Mace, the Lord Treasurer ; on his right and left and behind several Lords, as the Lord President of the Council, Lord Privy Seal, etc., all pell mell. Thus they proceeded along the Inner Court up the Great Stairs of the Exchequer in the corner of the Palace Yard, by the Talley Court, down the Stone Steps into Westminster Hall, by the Common Pleas Bar, where my Lord Treasurer made his obeisance to the Judges of that Bench, so up towards the Chancery Bar, and about the middle of the Hall made two obeisances, one to the Lord Keeper sitting in the Court of Chancery, the other to the Court of Queen's Bench, whence they proceeded up the Hall into the Court of Chancery, the officers filing off at the bottom of the steps, except the Marshall of the Exchequer and the Sargeant-at-Mace, with the Lords, where he took the oaths to the Queen, after which he came back, with the

Lord Keeper on his right hand, and the said officers before him by the Common Pleas Bar, where they both made their reverences to the Judges, so up the Stone Stairs into the Exchequer. The Barons being sat, my Lord Keeper went into the Court, placing himself on the right hand ot the Lord Chief Baron ; the Lord Treasurer was by the Marshall, and his own Sargeant conducted to the outside of the Bar, with the Sargeant-at-Mace on his left, when my Lord Keeper made a neat speech, signifying his Lordship's great abilities —that he had two offices, that of Lord High Treasurer by delivery of the Staff, and that of Treasurer of the Exchequer by Patent ; after which my Lord's Patent was read by one of the Clerks of the King's Remembrancer's Office Then his Lordship was conducted into the Court, where was a cushion provided, on which he knelt whilst the oaths of his respective officers were administered to him by the Lord Keeper. After which he was conducted to his place on the left of the Lord Keeper, and his patent delivered to him by the Lord Keeper ; which done, the Lord Keeper departed the Court, and the Lord Treasurer sat to hear motions some little time, after which he departed the Court, when he should have taken possession of the King's Remembrancer's Office, Treasurer's Remembrancer, Pipe, and other offices on that side of the Exchequer before he walked thence ; but he was conducted in the same order, accompanied to the Talley Court, where were placed cushions for him in the middle thereof, and two for the Chamberlains on each side by the Block, the two Deputy Chamberlains in each corner, the Lord Halifax, Talley-writer, and his Clerks on the right hand below the Senior Deputy Chamberlain ; the Deputy Clerk of the Pells, and his Clerk below the Junior Deputy Chamberlain ; then the Usher of the Exchequer just within the door, and the Talley-cutter without the Court, the Chancellor of the Exchequer on the Lord Treasurer's left, several Dukes and Earles round the Court, the Barons of the Exchequer on the outside of the Bar with the Attorney and Solicitor-General. When all were come in, a Bill was thrown down from the Tellers' offices, a Talley prepared, writ on, struck, and examined by the proper officers ; then his Lordship withdrew thence after having had the great keys of the Treasury presented to him by the Auditor, and he delivered them to him again ; then he went into the Auditors', Pells', and Tellers' offices, and viewed the cash in the last of them, the Barons of the Exchequer, Attorney and Solicitor, with the Dukes, Earles, etc., attending him to each office ; after which he went back again to the other side of the Exchequer to take possession of the several offices there, which he should have done before he came to the Receipt side, and after returned to his house.'

In the middle of the eighteenth century we find the duties and the manners and customs of the Exchequer officials still unchanged. They were now somewhat given to political discussions amongst themselves, and they were even contributors to the ministerial press. Naturally they shone in the clubs of the coffee-houses, and they were still more at home in those of the taverns of the later Georgian period. In most cases they were the deputies of the holders of political sinecures. They had no interest in, or responsibility for, their official work, except as a means of accumulating fees, and they openly devoted themselves to the pursuit of trade as their serious occupation.

There exists a collection of official and private papers for this period, of the same nature as the Fanshawe correspondence, already described, and ranging in date between 1735 and 1770, which give much curious information on the subject of official life at the Exchequer. Indeed, the papers in question once belonged to two generations of officers, and contained drafts of their political and poetical effusions (the latter being mostly designed for convivial occasions), and accounts of their private speculations.

Sometimes these rough drafts are merged in the

accounts in a way that is rather compromising to their former owners. In one case an official writes to his departmental chief to excuse himself from attendance on the ground that he has been 'ever since ye frost not able to get rid of a painfull rheumatism in my arm wch has now gradually weakened it . . . and such an attendance under my own present disorders, together with my own dayly sittings, would really be too much for me.' This draft contains the following remarkable endorsement :

2 quarts wanting.

2 gallons and 3 quarts of ————* melted in each barrel.

Taken out of both barrels—2 gallons, which filled 9 bottles and a $\frac{1}{4}$, and 2 gallons filled 2 French ditto, and 3 gallons which filled 13 bottles and above an $\frac{1}{2}$—19 gallons and $\frac{1}{2}$.

		£	s.	d.
Rum -	-	11	2	6
Oranges	-	1	1	6
Sugar	-	1	1	0
		13	5	0
		9	15	0
		3	10	0

In fact, however, this liberal provision of wine and punch was not intended, as might at first appear, as a cure for the rheumatism. One at least of these dignified public servants combined the business of a wine-merchant with his official

* Illegible.

employment, and the accounts and memoranda relative to his transactions are highly interesting, and even instructive, for economic or statistical purposes. The officer in question, and one of his colleagues with whom he was related, were burgesses of a small Essex seaport, doubtless in connection with their wine-business ; but their official residence was at Westminster, where Mill-bank also afforded facilities for the unshipping of pipes of claret and awms of old hock, hogsheads of cider, and, above all, casks of rum for the manufacture of shrub, which seems to have been their speciality. The extent of their business may be gathered from the fact that they provided three gross of quart bottles at one time.

Two more documents may be cited here in support of this view of the jovial period of the Exchequer in the last century. The first of these is a card of invitation in the following terms :

'Mr. Goff and Mr. Pearce, Chief Burgesses of Westminster for the year ensuing, present their Compliments to Abraham Farley, Esq', and Hope to have the Honour of his Company to Dine with them and the Burgesses at the King's Arms Tavern, in New Palace Yard, to-morrow the 15th Inst., it being the Day they are Sworn into their Office.

'Dinner to be on Table at 3 o'Clock.

'*April* 14, 17—.'

The guest whose pleasant company was solicited by the worthy burgesses on this occasion was a deputy chamberlain of the Exchequer, and a well-known, though apparently very convivial, antiquary, since the next document under notice appears, from external evidence, to allude to his promotion. It is curious in itself as indicative of the social tone of the Exchequer officers at the time, a curious contrast to the reliques of mediæval clerks, such as the *Dialogus* and the Red Book on the one hand, and to the dignified and practical character of the Elizabethan correspondence on the other.

‘ *Remonstrance of the Lower House of the Exchequer Feast to the Upper House.*

‘Forasmuch as the Gentlemen of the Upper House have of their own meer motion thought fit to call one of our Brethren up to their own Right Worshipfull House, and have thereby given occasion to very great Heart-burning and discontent amongst us; the whole body of the Lower House being justly alarm’d at so partial and unprecedented a proceeding, highly injurious to our Honour, as well as destructive of our rights and privileges, do, with all humility, take the liberty to remonstrate against such an extraordinary stretch of the Prerogative, and,

‘ 1st. We beg leave to observe that the said proceeding is unprecedented, and utterly contrary to ancient usage, there never having been an instance of a person thus called up, but where he happened to be distinguished wth the Honourable office of Justice of the Peace for the City and Liberty of Westminster.

' 2dly. That it deprives the Lower House of a most facetious and witty Member, which is greatly detrimental to Us, and can be of little advantage to the Upper House, wch so notoriously abounds with men of Wit and Humour.

3rdly. That it robs us of the almost only wealthy member of our body. And here we must crave leave to represent that tho' we have peaceably and wth a becoming Resignation submitted to the ordinary endeavours which have been used that there might not be a wealthy person among Us, yet in Duty to the Upper House who may in consequence be affected hereby, as well as in justice to ourselves, who are immediately so affected, we can by no means neglect to warn them of the fatal effects which we dread from such an extraordinary step.

' 4thly. That some of our body have absented from the Feast for several years past, on Account (as there is Cause to suspect) of ill Usage from particular Members of the other House, who in Despite to them, have lived to a very unreasonable Age, and we have great reason to apprehend that many others will withdraw themselves on this occasion to the Utter Ruin and Depopulation of the Lower House.

' 5thly. That if this shou'd be the Consequence (as seems to Us unavoidable) we shall be thereby render'd incapable of supporting the necessary expence of Our Meetings, which will deprive the Upper House of that homage wch we at every such time so cheerfully pay them, unless they shou'd please of their wonted generosity to bestow upon us the Charity that has hitherto been so constantly apply'd to the putting poor Children out Apprentices. We entreat your Permission, Most Grave Chiefs, to offer this our Humble Remonstrance to your serious Consideration, not doubting but you will of your profound Depth, very weighty Judgment and unsearchable Wisdom provide for the safety and emolument of your Faithful Vassals.'

Abraham Farley was the last Exchequer official of the old school whose name and occupations are entered in the Black Book of the Exchequer, the second of the two great precedent books of that ancient court. A transition period follows, characterized by reforms in its establishment and procedure, which culminated in the sweeping changes of the first years of the reign of William IV.

CHAPTER V.

THE CHESS-GAME.

ON the morrow of the Close of Easter, or on that of the Feast of St. Michael (the opening days of the working terms of the always short official year), the business of the Exchequer was in full operation.

If any modern could have peered through the woollen hangings or the flaxen drapery of the mullioned windows, into the great chamber where the barons sat as arbiters of the mimic warfare between treasurer and accountant, the strange sight would have been presented to his eyes of a score or so of grave and reverend officials, for the most part ecclesiastics, seated on low benches, round what might at first sight appear to be a billiard-table, with a dark cloth curiously patterned. In this last object he would have recognised the famous Exchequer-table, which has given its name both to the apartment and to the revenue, much as the decorated ceiling of another chamber is supposed to have suggested the name for a later tribunal—the Star Chamber.

The central object of the chamber, then, was a table ten feet long by five in width, bordered by a ledge four inches high and covered with dark russet cloth, divided into squares by intersecting lines, probably marked out with chalk, forming columns and spaces of account, within each of

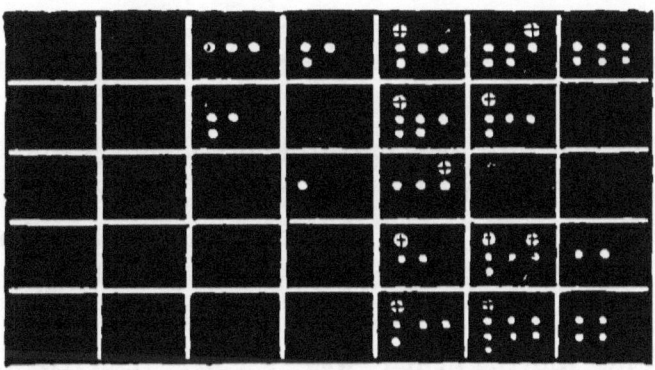

Fig. 19.—The Chess-board with the Pieces ' set.'

which a sum deposited had a certain numerical value according to its position towards the left hand of the reckoner, the column furthest to the right being for pence, the next shillings, the next pounds, and the remaining spaces scores, hundreds, and thousands of pounds respectively.

Around this chess-board sat the officials and their subordinates. At the head of the board, in the middle, the president or justiciar. To his

8—2

left the chancellor, by virtue of his office. Beside him the constable, next the two chamberlains, according to seniority, and last of this bench the marshal.

On the second bench, along the left side of the table, sat first the clerk of the chamberlains, with the counterparts of the tallies ready for use. Below him a few subordinates, and such courtiers as might attend by the king's wish. At about half-way down the table's length sat the calculator, and at the end of the bench the clerk of the rolls.

On the third bench to the president's right sat usually the treasurer, below him his scribe with the great roll; next the latter the chancellor's scribe with the counterpart of the great roll, and at his elbow the chancellor's clerk, or his deputy.

The fourth bench was usually reserved for accountants and their suites, who thus faced the president. On settles round the walls were grouped the accountant's debtors or creditors, as the case might be, armed with their private vouchers for the debts paid by them at the Exchequer through its officer (in case the latter should attempt to shift the responsibility for some deficit upon them), together with any other persons interested in the proceedings.

In one aspect these bishops, knights and chamberlains, in their robes of scarlet or black, with their subordinates grouped round them, might be taken to represent the greater pieces of the game with their attendant pawns, and this resemblance has had an undoubted share in suggesting an allegorical description of the proceedings. But apart from this similitude, a more immediate likeness to the chess-game was apparent in the arrangement of the board itself.

The game of chess at the Exchequer, according to its most approved etymology, is clearly not named after a ' ludus scaccarii,' the game, that is, played on a chequered board, but from the ' ludus scaccorum *sive* latrunculorum,' from *schach*—a dummy or counterfeit presentation—in the German, whence, coming West, it found its way into our vocabulary through the neo-Latin and official Norman-French, adopting later still a classical form.

It is most essential to grasp the significance of this origin of the word 'Exchequer,' which may, in the widest sense, be interpreted as the chamber wherein stood the table employed for the ' ludus computatorum,' or ' game of money-counters.' The form of this table having been already described, it remains now to give some account of the ' men,' or counters, which supplied the material for that mimic contest which was waged between the treasurer, with his staff, and the sheriff, or other accountant.

The chessmen of the Exchequer game were in one aspect the counters or dummy coins which, in their different sizes, colours, and combination, represented the actual specie coming into, or disbursed at, the treasury ; just as the bishops, knights, and pawns of the chess-game proper took the place of actual combatants, having certain strategic parts assigned to them, defined and limited by the laws of the play. The bullion actually received, or which remained to be accounted for, was also represented by a subsidiary set of chessmen, so to speak ; namely, by the tallies which stood for the cash payments already made upon his account by the sheriff, and by the vouchers or receipts which represented other sums disbursed by him on account of the crown, together with the corresponding warrants or mandates by which such disbursements had been authorized or allowed respectively, as the case might be.

The tallies proper in use at the Exchequer were a primitive form of chirograph or indented writing, recommended by their superior durability, from being composed of seasoned wood instead of parchment or paper, an advantage fully borne out by the perfect condition of such as have survived, on which every mark made by the knife stands out as clean and true as on the day when it was cut by the chamberlain's sergeant more than 600 years ago.

These rude memoranda were indeed invaluable auxiliaries of the hard-worked official staff of the Exchequer of Receipt. The high-born or well-to-do, yet often illiterate, sheriff of the crown, who came before the barons with his profer during Easter term, had but to pay in his treasure and take an acknowledgment in the shape of a small piece of wood inscribed with a figure-writing intelligible at a glance to the meanest comprehension. Then when he returned at Michaelmas to conclude his annual account, this indestructible voucher was readily forthcoming from his wallet to be compared, or rather matched, with its official counterpart. Or the same process was continued lower down the scale, the sheriff delivering to the king's debtors a tally of receipt on which he was bound to acquit them at the Exchequer.

Usually, however, tallies proper were only 'struck' at the Exchequer, and against the principal accountants ; the subsidiary or provincial 'tallies' being indented writings of receipt such as were delivered by agents of the crown to local producers, whose corn or cattle had been 'bought' or 'taken' for the king's use. It sometimes happened, too, that tallies came into the Exchequer through the department devoted to the financial superintendence of the Jews, the most ancient specimens surviving being of this nature.

The official definition of a tally was as follows :

A narrow shaft of box, willow, hazel, or other hard wood was shaped more or less square with the knife, and cut to the length of eight or nine inches, being allowed to taper somewhat at one extremity. On the obverse of this shaft was cut the principal sum in one bold notch, and no more. Then on the reverse surface were cut the subsidiary numerals of the sum required to be inscribed, with a suitable interval between each denomination. Moreover, the notches which represented figures of greatest value were always cut at the thickest end of the shaft ; those of least value towards the thinnest end.

Thus £1,000 was cut in one deep notch, of the width of a man's palm, along the upper side of the tally ; £100, when that was the highest figure present, was likewise cut alone on that side, but with a notch no wider than a thumb-mark ; £20 was cut in the same way as broad as the little finger ; and £1 with as deep a notch as would contain a barley-corn. Shillings and pence, on the other hand, were either cut on the lower side, when the above figures were present, or they might be placed on either side, when the sum was below the value of a pound.

It was permitted, however, to cut half of the value of any sum above one pound on the same side with a single deep incision, that is to say, without removing any of the wood ; or it might be set forth at length, if preferred, on the other side.

On the two remaining faces of the shaft was a superscription setting forth the object and nature of the tally, and sometimes even its amount.

A very perfect specimen of a tally is figured here with twelve slanting notches (not unlike the teeth of a saw) cut from right to left, beginning at the bluntest end of the shaft. Each of these

Fig 20.

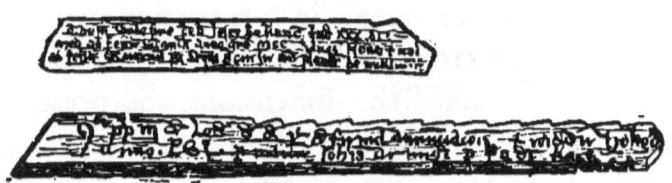

Fig. 21.

Exchequer Tallies.

notches represents a pound, and they are followed on the reverse side by the residue of the sum, consisting of 4s. 4d. The superscription states that this is a tally against the receiver of the royal manor of Ledcombe (Berks) for rent due at Lady Day in the fifty-sixth year of Henry III.

It is possible to pronounce this to be the official counterpart of the original tally, because the remaining half, handed to the accountant, would have possessed a 'handle,' or undivided base, since all tallies were cut down to a cross section, where they were divided into two unequal halves, the longer one called the 'stalk,' and the shorter one the 'leaf.' It is well known, of course, that when the accountant presented his 'stalk,' or 'counterfoil,' at Michaelmas, it was spliced on to the leaf or 'foil' in official custody, and carefully preserved by the marshal. Though in the days of Richard, Bishop of London, nine inches was length enough to enable any reasonable account to be entered on a tally, yet in later times the size of the shafts was increased in proportion with the revenue of the crown, till the tally of the present century had attained the dimensions, and presented somewhat the appearance, of one of the wooden swords of the South Sea Islanders.

In a typical case, therefore, the sheriff who paid in advance at the Receipt of the Exchequer upon his account, received credit for the same by a 'tally' delivered to him then and there, with the amount of his advance duly recorded upon it. At the same time the officials kept in hand the 'counter-tally' in the shape of a symmetrical half of the whole tally, which had been cleft for that purpose, in the same manner as a chirograph, or indented writing. It is worth notice that the technical name of the accountant's indenture was 'schacchia' — 'scaccus' or 'scach,' that is — the dummy of the mass of silver now finally deposited in the treasury, or consigned to the Mint if occasion required.

Of course, if the accountant were allowed for a sum not actually paid into the Receipt *in specie*, but disbursed instead by him in the king's service, the voucher produced by him, that the assignment in point had really been concluded, should correspond with the mandate authorizing such assignment, which latter record, laid up with the tallies themselves amongst the archives of the marshal's department, already represented so much more specie, here supposed only to exist, and which would eventually, through other channels, find its way into the treasury, or go to balance the rolls of the issue and receipt sides of the revenue. In fact, there can be but little doubt that these dummies, whether counter-tallies or mandates preponderated amongst them, formed the chief assets of the sheriff when he stood before the barons with the sum of his reckoning on the morrow of St. Michael.

Just as the tally stood for money in this official chess-game, so the paper denominations of pounds, shillings, and even marks, both of gold and silver, were in themselves dummies of the single coin in general use during the halcyon days of the Exchequer. That coin was the silver penny, described therefore, with equal justice, either as 'denarius' or 'nummus,' and it was an obvious convenience to be able to denote its aggregate value by a single symbol for each of the unwieldy sums that were commonly presented upon the board ; especially, too, when such symbols needed only to be multiplied within themselves to discover the value of any inclusive sum.

The counters in use at the Exchequer were coins of a size and appearance easily distinguishable from current sterling money. For this purpose besants, or the depreciated 'solidi' of the Eastern Empire, were in requisition at an early date. These 'Byzantines' were frequently received at the Exchequer in the fines paid by the alien merchants, and were sent either as bullion to the Mint, or retained for use as counters. Their intrinsic value for the latter service was estimated in the early part of the thirteenth century as equal to 1s. 9d. sterling. Besides these there was another gold counter available, the 'obolus,' which might be either a weight equal to twelve grains, or a half-noble when these were coined. In reality, however, the obolus was the specific half of some current denomination, without itself possessing any recognised circulation. This fiction has given rise to several difficulties in the study of early finance. Madox, for instance, confesses himself unable to comprehend the meaning of the entry 'unam marcam auri de obolo Musce' in the fine of a Jewish merchant. But it is quite clear that this fine of some £6 sterling is an equivalent for half a pennyweight or twelve grains of *musk* (that most costly of perfumes) bargained for by the crown, just as it accepted falcons, or hunting-dogs, or furs under special circumstances.

It is evident, then, that a half-pennyweight might be recognised at the Exchequer, and at the same time could be conveniently employed for ordinary purposes as a counter. At any rate, no 'noble' was in existence at the date when the *Dialogus* was written, and that treatise makes particular mention of an 'obolus auri' used as a counter. It seems, indeed, that in the time of the good Bishop Richard, of London, both a gold and silver obolus were used as official ready-reckoners, the former standing for £10—that is, for 2,400 pence—the latter for 10s., or 120 pence. Naturally, the silver obolus, weighing but twelve grains, would appear only half the size of the sterling penny of twenty-four grains, and would thus escape confusion with it, just as silver-metal coins of about half the size of a threepenny-piece are often used as counters in round-games at cards ; and as, *per contra*, the use of the 'Hanover sovereign' for a like purpose once gave rise to such serious abuses.

Still later in the reign of Edward II., besides the 'Byzantines' already mentioned, we find Venetian 'shillings' in chief favour at the Exchequer as counters, on account of their superior size and weight. The intrinsic value of these coins was estimated at 1s. 6d. sterling. The distinguishing feature of counters was therefore, now, an exaggerated instead of a minute size. Let us suppose the *onus* of the accountant's charge to amount to £199 13s. 4d., it may be assumed that some £100 of this has been already paid in, say, in six tallies, or allowed for, perhaps, by an equal number of mandates. These tallies and mandates, as we have seen, are so many dummies marshalled on the accountant's side, not actually placed on the board ; but, from their evidence, the counters are arranged in the requisite numerical combination, as a counterbalance to the treasurer's statement, within the space nearest to the computator. When the whole sum of the sheriff's assets is at length exhausted, there is a pause, whilst the evidence in his favour is being further scrutinized : the tallies produced by his servants are compared with the authentic foils, and his vouchers with the mandates filed among the marshal's county *collectanea*. All these proving satisfactory, or satisfaction being exacted in default, a series of rapid exchanges (in chess parlance) follows, or, in the concise language of the *Dialogus*, ' fit simplex subtractio,' and the game is won and lost, or left merely drawn.

To explain the *rationale* of this conclusion we must refer to the problem figured at p. 115. In this diagram the treasurer's counters are arranged in the upper spaces to represent a sum of £374 10s. 6d., the column furthest to the right representing pence, the next to the left shillings, the next pounds, the next twenties of pounds, and the last hundreds of pounds. In the same way, in the lower spaces the accountant's principal assets are shown in the usual combinations, the result being a deficit, as figured on the bottom line, of £14 17s. 4d.

We will now search for the key to this formidable looking cryptogram. In the first place, we must premise that the system in question is a decimal one. We were prepared for this discovery by the statement made in the *Dialogus* with reference to the practice of placing a counter in every tenth place for intervening units in the second and third columns or principal columns of account. For odd units the early computator would have recourse to sterling coins, either separately or in combination. But at a comparatively early period it may be clearly gathered that counters only in combination were exclusively used.

To begin with the pence column. As by far the majority of sums in the addition of these denominations, owing chiefly to the conventional quotation of marks, left a remainder over of 4 or 8, it is unusual to find any other combination of 'dots' to express pence to the amount of 11 or less. These, then, were figured by four dots at the angles of a square, and three dots at the points of a triangle, respectively.

The units above 8, however, might be figured on occasion by dots placed below the base of the triangle, as

Remainders of pence under 8 were easily represented by an aggregation of 'dots' in the usual way, as exemplified in the following method of figuring numbers from 1 to 20 :

One	= ●	= unit.
Two	= ● ●	= 1 + 1.
Three	= ● ● ●	= 2 + 1.
or	= ● ● over ●	= 2 + 1.
Four	= ● ● ● ●	= 1 + 1 + 1 + 1.
or	= ● ● ● over ●	= 3 + 1.
Five	= ● ● ● over ● ●	= 3 + 2.
Six	= ● ● ● over ● ● ●	= 3 + 3.
or	= ● ● over ● ● over ● ●	= 2 + 2 + 2.
Seven	= ● ● ● over ● ● ● over ●	= 3 + 3 + 1.

or	=	$= 2 + 5.$*
Eight	=	$= 3 + 5.$*
Nine	=	$= 4 + 5.$*
Ten	=	$= 5 + 5.$*
Eleven	=	$= 6 + 5.$*
Twelve	=	$= 2 + 10.$†
Thirteen	=	$= 3 + 10.$†
Fourteen	=	$= 4 + 10$ †
Fifteen	=	$= 5 + 10.$†
Sixteen	=	$= 6 + 10.$†
Seventeen	=	$= 7 + 10.$†
Eighteen	=	$= 3 + 5 + 10.$‡
Nineteen	=	$= 4 + 5 + 10.$‡

* Semi-decimal point to the right above the unit line.
† Decimal point to the left above the unit line.
‡ Decimal and semi-decimal points combined above the unit line.

It will be obvious what an economy of time and labour was effected by this simple expedient. In the case of £18, for instance, the 4,320 pence contained therein were actually pictured on the board and accounted for to the dullest of accountants by the clearest ocular demonstration ; and yet, by means of the admirable system of the Exchequer, not one of these 4,320 coins needed to be produced, their existence being satisfactorily proven by the comparison of two little bits of notched stick, and their sum counted, as it were, on the fingers, by the combination of five metal counters in duplicate.

The reader will understand that 20s. was figured in the third column as a unit ; and £21, £101, £1,001, £10,001, in the same way, in their respective columns, also as units. Given this key, the inquiring spirit will readily be enabled to work out any possible combination that could be presented upon the Exchequer chess-board.

The further question certainly arises as to the connection of these later ' pen and ink dots ' with the counters of the early Exchequer. Here we are confronted with an absence of early instances, due, no doubt, to the employment of actual counters down to a comparatively late date. Therefore, it is not till the Tudor period that we meet with the later system, though isolated instances are reported from records of the fifteenth century. On this account, perhaps, there has been some disposition evinced to assign these 'pen and ink dots' to the period of the general introduction of Arabic numerals, coinciding, perhaps, with the use of the Eastern 'abacus.' But, on the other hand, we may suppose that such symbolism by the way of picture-writing was practised amongst most nations at an early age of official development. At least, we know that this was the case in England, and the connection between the 'game of counters' played at the Exchequer in the days of the author of the *Dialogus*, and the later 'pen and ink dots' of the fifteenth or sixteenth centuries, is obviously complete from the description of the treatise in question. Moreover, both systems were exclusively used in the Exchequer, a fact which may be illustrated in a somewhat remarkable manner. 'Pen and ink dots' sometimes occur amongst the state papers of the sixteenth century, but in every case the calculator has been found to be an official of the Exchequer. Thus Lord Treasurer Burleigh sometimes made use of them, by force of habit, for the purpose of checking a commercial schedule in his other capacity of prime minister. The latest instance of these 'pen and ink dots' that has hitherto been found is of the somewhat abnormal date of 1676 ; here again in an Exchequer account, and

9—2

carefully preserving the system described in 1177. The entry is as follows:

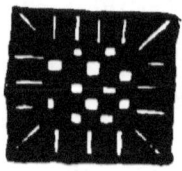 $= £4,438$ 10s. 4d.

Thus it may be safely concluded that the system of reckoning by counters, as described in the *Dialogus*, was consistently preserved down to a comparatively modern date—' *Secundum consuetum cursum Scaccarii, non legibus aritmeticis.*'

And now the 'game' has been opened. The treasurer speaking first, slowly and distinctly,

Fig. 22.   Fig. 23.

The Symbols of the Exchequer.

asks his adversary if he is ready to render his account. The latter replies in the affirmative, and is immediately challenged upon the first item of his reckoning. Hereupon a general commotion ensues. The clerks turn the membranes of their rolls to compare the entries of previous years, and the chamberlains serjeants heap upon the table rouleaux of silver, counter-tallies, and warrants, representing the accountant's credit in the treasury. Then the calculator, rising in his place, prepares to make the moves of the game as they are dictated from the contents of the great roll.

The sum of each separate entry of the farm of the county being announced, he leans over and arranges on the side farthest from him the amount quoted, in specie or in counters, within the appropriate columns. Next he sorts out the credit before him into heaps in the same columns below this dummy treasure, and, when everything is complete, subtracts pence from pence, shillings from shillings, and pounds from pounds, till the corresponding pieces on both sides are exhausted by the exchange. Then, unless the accountant is quit, so much as is left on either side represents the advantage or loss of each respectively, the deficit being made good or the surplus being allowed, as it might befall.

Meanwhile, the tallies held by the sheriff's servants have been carefully compared with the foils preserved in the Exchequer, to guard against a forgery, or even a slip of the knife, and woe betide him if any such flaw be discovered, for then he would be forthwith handed over to the marshal for safe custody in the Fleet, unless he could fasten the fraud upon his deputy or attorney.

And so the contest is slowly waged, the piles of silver, gold, and metal counters, sticks and scrolls, being marshalled, advanced, and swept off the board, just as the pieces or pawns of the real game might have been played, till the account of the farm is concluded, and the mimic warfare terminates in a truce between the parties for another six months at least.

CHAPTER V..

1. *The Great Roll.*

THE Treasurer's Roll, which figures in the above description of the Michaelmas audit of the sum of the Sheriff's account, was that commonly known as the great or annual roll of the Exchequer. The still more familiar appellation of pipe roll is a later and less exact synonym for the authoritative enrolment compiled by the treasurer's scribe. The etymology of the word 'pipe' remains a subject of discussion to the present day among antiquaries. The name may have been applied from the obvious resemblance of these compact rolls to sections of a tubular drain or pipe. Again, an origin can be found for the simile in the favourite comparison of the public treasury to a reservoir, into which every branch of the revenue flows through one main conduit—'quasi per ductum (seu *pipam*) aquæ'— as described in the following curious notice:

'The Platforme of the Exchequer.

'The best and comon received opinion is that our Ancestors in the Institucon of this Court (for the better and safe conveyance of the revenue into his Ma^{tes} Coffers) tooke their plott from an *Aqueduct*. That as water is derived from many springes to heades, and from heades guided into a pipe, and by that carried into the Cesterne of a greate house or pallace, where it is to bee expended accordinge to the necessitie and use of every office. Soe, this silver streame, growing out of divers natures, might bee drawne from its springes, wch are the severall Courtes from whence it ariseth, to certaine heades, from thence collected into one pipe, and by that conveyed into the Cesterne, wch is his Ma^{tes} receipte.

'The conceipt of this was, that it might not bee left in any man's curtesy to deceive the Kinge.

'For if the pipe received in his due at the one end, it would be easilie comptrolled, seeing the Cisterne joyneth to the other.

'Hereuppon that office in the Exchequer, called the Pipe, first obteyned and to this day holdeth its name.'*

The great roll being, as we have learnt, the official register of all debts of the crown answerable at the Exchequer (just as the Domesday

* From a MS. communicated by the late Mr. Walford Selby.

Survey was the unalterable evidence of the extent of demesnes, from which this annual revenue of the sovereign was mainly derived), a new edition had to be annually prepared, embracing such alterations as were necessitated by the varying conditions of the county farms and the extraordinary or casual revenue estimated for the current year.

As the Exchequer itself was a court of supreme jurisdiction in all matters relating to the revenue of the crown, in which (technically speaking) the king was plaintiff and his debtors defendants, the greatest care was exercised from the earliest times to ensure the infallibility of its decisions upon all questions as to facts. The means to this end were, firstly, the permanent appointment of a great official, the treasurer ; and, secondly, the committal of the great roll and all its appurtenances into his sole custody. Thus the crown was enabled to rely with almost absolute certainty upon the accuracy of its official instrument in the case of any financial detail in dispute, from the knowledge that every part of it was compiled from the dictation and under the immediate supervision of an official who was also one of the foremost scholars and statesmen of his day ; for, as we have seen, the scribe of the great roll was seated at the Exchequer table by the treasurer's side, writing at his dictation and under his immediate supervision. Not only so, but a further safeguard was employed by the crown in the designation of its chancellor to represent the equitable jurisdiction of the sovereign at the Exchequer as a foil to official callousness or rapacity. This latter official may have put in appearance only on certain high days, but his watchful clerk was always at his post, on the other side of the scribe of the antigraph, who transcribed faithfully from the treasurer's scribe, the last named now working under the double check of his own chief and of the chancellor's representative.

Not content with these precautions, an additional scribe sat, in the early days of the Exchequer, with a third roll, under the direction of an extraordinary representative of the king—the famous 'Magister Thomas Brunus,' a Sicilian refugee, reputed to be without an equal in Europe for his knowledge of statecraft. He, therefore, attended to watch the proceedings on behalf of the king, while his scribe made notes of the points affecting the royal prerogative. The latter was present also at the Exchequer of Receipt, to check the entries of all returns and disbursements there made.

In reality, it was due to the active presence of one and all of these great officials at the Exchequer that the severity of its financial system was acquiesced in by the nation during the reigns of Henry II. and his sons.

For the preparation of the great roll, the treasurer's scribe was required to provide himself with suitable parchment out of the five shillings annually allowed him for the whole service of his office in this particular. The material, as we have seen, was bound to be of sheep-skins, so selected for their superior size that two membranes might suffice for the length of each rotulet, while their normal width was to be fifteen inches. On each of these rotulets lines were ruled, ample space being left between each, and also between the top and bottom of the joint membranes. Then, on the top line, were inscribed the names of the shires or bailiwicks whose issues were first in order to be answered, according to the groups under which they happened to fall, and below these the first name of the group was boldly written in the centre of the membrane.

At the commencement of the following line the accountant's name figured as rendering an account of the farm of that shire. Then, at the end of this statement, the words 'In Thesauro' were put and a space left blank.

On the next line were entered the fixed alms in like form. Next, the fixed disbursements made by him, with their amount, together with the lands granted by the crown within the county proper, were entered in the same manner. Lastly were entered the casual disbursements made by the accountant out of his farm in the king's service, as well as the necessary expenses incurred by him, chiefly in the execution of his legal functions. Thus :

A—— Shire, et B—— Shire, et C—— Shire.

A—— Shire.

The sheriff renders his account of the farm of A——shire.

In the Treasury.

> And in fixed alms.
> And in fixed tithes.
> And in fixed payments.
> And in lands granted.
> And in payments by the king's writ or otherwise.

The whole of the above entries may be classified thus :

(1) The farm of the county which forms the accountant's charge.
(2) His allowance in the five subsequent entries, subdivisible, as :
(i.) Fixed allowances, namely, alms, tithes, liveries, and lands.
(ii.) Casual disbursements (authorized by the king's writ).
(iii.) Casual disbursements (authorized by the custom of the Exchequer).

Below this statement of the charge and allowance for the farm of the county was entered that relating to the farm of purprestures and escheats; the state of the sheriff's account herein being specified as for so much paid into the treasury, and his quittance or indebtedness thereupon, as the case might be, thus :

Of purprestures and escheats.

The same sheriff renders his account of the farm of the purprestures and escheats ———. In the treasury ; and he is in debt, or is quit.

After this came the similar statement for the issues of the royal forests, unless these were already assigned for the fixed allowances in the body of the county, thus :

The same sheriff renders his account of the rent of the wood of —— or the forest of ——
In the Treasury.

Next were entered pleas and conventions of all sorts ; the former being nominally judicial fines or amerciaments, and the latter oblations, tendered usually for a specific purpose, the sheriff answering for all issues from the Danegeld, etc., or from murders within the hundred ; and as to the rest, the individuals charged therewith, in their own names, thus :

The same sheriff renders his account of the Danegeld.
The same sheriff renders his account of a murder-fine of——
A. B. renders his account (or the same sheriff renders his account for A. B.) of or for ——

In each of the above instances, the charge was usually answered in one of the following forms :

(1) In the treasury—and he is quit.

(2) In the treasury—and he owes.

(3) Expended by the king's (writ or custom of the Exchequer).

(4) Pardoned by the king's writ.

The statement of the sheriff's account usually concluded with the entries of these pleas and oblations, all the recent items of which were consolidated under the comprehensive title of 'New Pleas and New Conventions' as a distinct heading. Moreover, their position was somewhat an anomalous one, the sheriff being responsible only for the due collection of the sums in charge, and each individual charged being severally allowed, or continuing to be indebted in his own name. Hence, these separate entries are more fitly regarded as an appendix to the sheriff's personal account, forming a register of the king's debtors for whom *collectively* he answered.

As soon as the last entry of the assessed or casual charges outside the 'body' of the county had been filled in, and certified as acquitted, or otherwise, the sum of the main account remained to be taken in the manner before described— namely, by a final test of the specie or credits paid in, followed by a display of the result of the net charge, and corresponding allowance, in counters upon the board by the calculator.

Then a subtraction of the lower lines of 'chess-

men ' from the top line left the result manifest to
the eyes of all present in the chamber. If the
charge and allowance balanced one another, the
scribe of the great roll, turning back to the initial
entry, filled in the blank left after the words
' In the Treasury,' with the amount paid into the
treasury, and wrote in bold characters at the end
of this first charge and allowance, that is to say,
below the allowance for customary disbursements,
the result as : 'And he is quit'; or, if the payment and allowances aforesaid did not satisfy the
charge, he wrote instead : 'And he is in debt———'
But if the accountant were actually to the good
on these transactions, the entry was made : ' And
he has a surplus of———.'

In this latter event, however, the excess usually
arose from the payments to assignees of the crown
beyond the amount of the farm of the county, in
which case no payment whatsoever was made ' In
the Treasury,' the form in question remaining
blank, or being omitted entirely.

The above form of entry of the various items of
the sheriff's charge and allowance, whether within
or without the ' body ' of the county, is, it must
be remembered, only the typical one in use at the
Exchequer in the early period. An examination
of the rolls will show that it varied, at times,
in many particulars ; but these variations, on the
other hand, will be found to be due chiefly to

omissions of certain of these normal entries, and to be in the main unimportant.

For example, an analysis of the Staffordshire account in the great roll for the fifth year of Henry II. shows as follows :

STAFFORDSHIRE.

Robert de Stafford renders his account for the farm of Staffordshire, and pays into the treasury £55 15s. 10d., blank, in two tallies, showing that he has already made a profer to that amount in cash at the Easter Exchequer, for which he will now be allowed.

(1) But he has also disbursed, recently, in fixed alms to the Templars 13s. 4d.

(2) [Here the entry for fixed tithes should have been made, but none such had been disbursed.]

(3) He has also disbursed 30s. and 5d. for the livery of the keeper of certain of the king's houses. [This, apparently, should have been specified as a fixed livery, and the entry should also have been commenced on a separate line.]

(4) He also craves allowance for certain lands granted out of his county, to the value of £48.

(5) And he has disbursed, by the king's writ, for work executed £25 2s. 4d., and as a gift to Geoffrey Marmion 20 marks. [These entries for disbursements by the king's writ should have been

commenced on a separate line, and at a slight distance below the preceding entries.]

(6) [Here should have followed the entries for disbursements made by virtue of his office, but none such had been made.]

The above entries constitute the charge and allowance of the sheriff for the 'body' of his county, and at the close of this, the principal portion of his account, appears the certificate of his quittance. We have now, therefore, to ascertain how this result was arrived at.

In the first place, the charge of the farm is not specified, either for this or any preceding year. We know, however, that the sheriff had made a profer of £55 15s. 10d., blank; and we also know that it was usual to pay in about half the total amount of a farm on such occasions; and we are able to calculate, further, that the total of the charge amounted to £112 7s. 11d., blank, for this and the following year.

Against this, he is allowed for 13s. 4d. in fixed alms; for £1 10s. 5d. in fixed livery; and £48 in lands granted; and for £38 9s. in disbursements by the king's writ—making a total allowance of £88 12s. 9d. But he is not actually allowed for £30 of the £48 for lands granted, because William de Beauchamp is charged with the same (and has been so charged, we discover, by the rolls since the beginning of the reign). This reduces the allowance to £58 12s. 9d., which acquits the account. How? Because this latter sum has to be *blanched*, being subject to a deduction of 12d. from a sum of £40 12s. 9d. disbursed by the king's writs. When it has been blanched the allowance should correspond nearly with the other half of the farm already paid in the profer, making two sums of £55 15s. 10d. and £56 12s. 1d., which being allowed, the one in two tallies, and the other in (supposed) dealbated bullion, added together will balance the charge of £112 7s. 11d. for the farm of the county.

Therefore, after each payment had been satisfactorily proved, the calculator would have arranged on the side of the table opposite to him the following combination in counters, and below that its duplicate (each being made up from the evidence of the Rotulus Exactorius), the former to represent the charge, and the latter the allowance of the accountant. Thus:

The remaining entries are those for Nova Placita et Novæ Conventiones—that is, pleas and conventions chargeable since or outside the last account. These, it will be seen, are all acquitted to the accountant as his summons is proceeded with ; and, except the last, they are all of the nature of conventions, namely, voluntary oblations as opposed to assessed issues of pleas. The last entry is probably for the issues of pleas of the crown, holden by Bertram de Verdun, whom we know (from later pipe rolls) was a famous justice of this reign. Here the sheriff pays in three tallies for £12, which he has delivered into the treasury in cash with his profer. He claims the king's writ of *Perdono*, laid up in the Exchequer, acquitting Bertram of twenty marks more, and he is indebted for Bertram in two marks, which the latter pays himself, and for which he is acquitted in the roll of the following year.

At the same time it should be remembered that the sheriff's allowance was also commonly figured on the board by the several sums which went to make up the total, these being added together and then subtracted from the top line of figures, or charge. It is also probable that a much larger deduction may have been made from every item of the allowance than has been here provided for, since the ' combustions ' of this and the earlier years of the reign are no longer extant.

BALANCE-SHEET

Of the Staffordshire Account of the Great Roll, 5 Henry II.

Dr.

	£	s.	d.
Farm of the county - - -	112	7	11
Blanching the allowances made to the sheriff out of the farm - (blank)	2	0	8
Issues of early pleas and conventions - - - - -	26	13	4
Issues of recent pleas and conventions - - - -	102	6	8
Total - -	243	8	7

Cr.

	£	s.	d.
Profer of the farm made before this account (represented by two tallies) -	55	15	10
Profer for the pleas of Bertram de Verdun (represented by three tallies) - (blank)			
Allowances out of the farm -	12	0	0
Paid into the treasury in cash -	58	12	9
Discharged by the king's writ -	99	6	8
-	16	6	8
Total - -	242	1	11

	£	s.	d.
Total charge -	243	8	7
Total allowance -	242	1	11
Balance against the accountant -	1	6	8

2. *The Summonses of the Exchequer.*

In the Exchequer chamber were assembled, at the opening of the two great sessions of the fiscal year, both parties interested in the audit of the revenues of the crown ; one (as it were) on the Bench, the other at the Bar. That is to say, the periodical summons served upon the sheriffs and debtors, at large, of the crown equally occasioned the meeting of the Barons for the despatch of the business in hand. The summons of the accountants to answer for the issues of the king's farms, debts, and casual revenue was thus the only motive for the session of the Exchequer, and the sole legal occasion for the same in early times. Hence we may account for the circumstance that only two sessions of the court were holden— namely, for the terms of Easter and Michaelmas —the two 'Exchequers,' as, in fact, they were called, of those respective dates. But in the intervening vocations, the official staff was not idle, being engaged in the arduous work of preparing the summonses of the sheriffs to the forthcoming ' Exchequer.'

For this purpose, the great roll was consulted by the treasurer, or by his clerk for him, who extracted therefrom, on the model of the entries of the preceding year, the charge of each accountant for the current financial period These

headings, when taxed by the Barons, were engrossed by the chancellor's clerk, and were then
ready to be issued for service on the provincial
accountants.

The form of the summons was that of a missive
patent ; on which account perfect accuracy of
detail and regularity of penmanship were essential,
to guard against evasion or forgery. Thus, no
cancelled or elided entries were permitted on the
patent, but all clerical errors were cleanly erased.
Still further to prevent the possibility of fraud, it
was the practice, at one time, to copy all summonses in duplicate, so that when the sheriff returned his summons at Michaelmas the latter
document might be compared with the rescript
remaining in the Exchequer, to make sure that it
had not been tampered with. In any case, however, the existence of the originals, from which
the summons was prepared, would have made the
destruction or forgery of the latter a suicidal act
on the part of the sheriff ; for from the authority
of Exchequer records there was no appeal,
and any discrepancy in an accountant's warrants
or tallies was not only disallowed, but heavily
punished as a presumptive fraud.

The summons, then, of the Exchequer was a
schedule of the headings of entries composing the
whole of the sheriff's charge for the current term.
This was derived from two official records : the

great roll, and the rolls of the justices' itinerant estreated into the Exchequer. In the first place, the king sent greeting to the sheriff by name, enjoining him, under certain pains, to be at the Exchequer on the day specified, and to have with him what was due from the farm of his county, or from the debtors of the crown, whose names were therein set forth, as recorded in the great roll.

Next, the debts assessed in the justices' rolls were extracted in due order, and the summons concluded with a fresh injunction to have all of the above forthcoming in specie, tallies, warrants, and vouchers, or any one of them. The summons was then attested at the Exchequer by the justiciar and constable, or two other officials, and delivered to the marshal, to be handed over by him, in turn, to the usher, for service in each county.

It was said that there were two sessions of the Exchequer, each convoked by a summons of the nature described above ; but it should be added that the form of the summons differed materially in either case. At the Easter sessions not the account itself of the sheriff was taken, but the view of his account only ; that is to say, he was summoned for half of his farm, and any other accessible credits, at the discretion of the officials or the pressing need of the crown.

The method by which these profers were

allowed to the accountant may be gathered from
the wording of the second or greater summons—
namely, that for the Michaelmas session.   He is
required, as we have seen, to have with him in
money, tallies, or writs, etc., all the items of
charge specified in that summons.   This plan of
payment supposes the existence of a previous
transaction, while at the same time superseding it ;
for, otherwise, the sheriff would make his payments at Michaelmas in cash, and would, moreover, having already answered the charge of the
Easter summons in like manner, have no further
concern on the score of the latter transaction.   In
fact, his responsibilities were not laid aside till the
whole sum of his annual charge was acquitted on
the following grounds:

Supposing that the sheriff were summoned for
a view of his farm of £200 at Easter, this would
necessitate a profer to be made by him of £100.
This he makes accordingly at the Easter Exchequer
in cash ; but is not yet acquitted for the same,
being only allowed for it by a tally struck for that
amount (the counter or foil of which is laid up at
the Receipt), or by the king's writ or writs
authorizing the disbursement of an equivalent
sum in the public service.

The sheriff having returned home with this
tally, receives shortly afterwards another summons,
that for the Michaelmas Exchequer, by which he

is required to answer the same sum of £200, regardless of his recent proffer. At the opening of the next term he betakes himself accordingly before the Barons, and pays in, *not* the clear £200, but £100 in cash and the other £100 in the tally (or warrant) before delivered to him, as the receipt for his profer (or disbursement), thus satisfying the command of the summons for payment to be made ' in money or in tallies,' etc.

It was expected of the sheriff, and so expressed in his summons, that, if a debtor of the Crown, for whom he was held to answer in his account, had no lands or goods in his bailiwick, but was known to have such in another county, a missive should be despatched by him to his brother official and delivered in the County Court, or some other public place, so that the debtor in question might have no opportunity (through a previous intimation) of fraudulently disposing of his possessions, but might be attached then and there where he stood in court to find security for the debt.

So, too, it was always understood that, if the fine or oblation, etc., of a debtor were assessed by the justices at a lower sum than should have been required of him, they were liable for the deficit, and therefore were charged by name with all such debts of the crown, in the first instance, in the great roll.

Thus we find A, the sheriff, answering for the pleas of B, the justice, who assesses the fine of C, the king's debtor, or the nominal defendant. Yet here B is the immediate bailee for C, though A renders the account for both.

A remaining point of procedure to be noticed is that oblations, tendered by individuals in the shape of hawks, were rarely entered in the Easter summons of the sheriff, as it would have been a useless expense to the crown to keep the birds in mew during the moulting period of the summer months, the royal hawking season extending from November till March.

In order to comply fully with the wording of the summons, the personal attendance of the sheriff was requisite at the Exchequer. He was required, also, to give notice by proclamation within his bailiwick of the date and place of summons, that his debtors might have an opportunity of watching his operations. On the appointed day, therefore, the sheriff appeared at the place where the Exchequer was holden, and presented himself to the president or treasurer. Then, saluting the Barons, he withdrew, to put in a similar appearance each day until his turn arrived for rendering his account. In default of such appearance he might be fined 100s. for the first day, £10 for the second and third days, and on the fourth was placed at the king's mercy. This meant that his goods were answerable by distress for the charge of his farm and debts, and his own person liable to be attached by the marshal for contempt.

The absence of the sheriff might, however, be excused on certain grounds — on account of sickness, for instance, which he must notify to the Barons ; or by virtue of the king's writ in his behalf addressed to the treasurer or Barons. In the former case he might despatch attorneys to render the account in his stead, provided they were qualified by relationship or rank. In all other cases, only his eldest son might answer for him, except by the king's writ. But in any case the cause of his absence must be a valid one.

3. *The Writs of the Exchequer.*

It was an accepted principle at the Exchequer that no part of the sovereign's treasure might be expended or allowed without the express sanction of the king's writ.

The former of these restrictions was obviously necessary to guard against the gravest abuses of extravagance, or even of peculation ; and hence no moneys passed into a subject's hands at the issue of the Exchequer without the authority of a royal warrant, in the shape of a writ of Liberate, for ordinary purposes tested at the Exchequer, to distinguish it from writs made in the king's court

—a distinction which was soon lost sight of. The following is a rare example of a writ 'for the issue of treasure' of the reign of Henry II. :

'Henry, by the grace of God, etc. To R., his treasurer, and William Malduit and Warin, son of Gerold, his chamberlains, greeting. Deliver out of my treasure 25 marks to the Brethren of the Charter House, being part of the 50 marks which I do yearly grant to them by my charter.

'Witness, William, of St. Mary's Church at Westminster.'

For the purposes of allowance to an accountant the existence of the king's writ was equally essential, though here this might be expressed in several different forms.

Thus, when the king's writ was made out at the Exchequer directing the accountant's acquittal for any sum expended by him in the public service, the scribe always made a rescript of the same, which was carefully laid up against the Michaelmas audit. Then, when the sheriff or other debtor of the crown claimed allowance for any item of his charge, by producing the king's writ, either directed to him, or issued on his behalf, before that allowance was made, the rescript at the Exchequer was compared with the original to guard against a forgery.

But in most cases of disbursements by the accountant, by the king's writ, a more complicated process had to be gone through. As stated above, the sheriff would claim allowance by producing the king's writ directed to or made out for him, but the nature of these two instruments differed widely.

The writ directed to the accountant by name was not an official, but an original writ, tested, that is, by the sovereign himself, and simply commanding the sheriff to pay so much, or provide such and such necessaries ' for the king's use' out of his farm ; adding at the close of the precept, ' and it shall be computed to you at the Exchequer.' Usually, too, he was required in this writ to make the provision in question ' by the view' of persons mentioned by name therein, who were, in most cases, agents of the crown, royal taskers, purveyors, and the like.

Now, when the sheriff cast the sum of his account at the Exchequer, he was not allowed for this disbursement or provision by merely producing his precept. He had first to prove the execution of the same, and also that he had done it satisfactorily ; for which purpose his ' viewers' were examined before the Barons on their oaths— an early form of sworn representation (for these viewers were at times local jurats) for purposes of imperial taxation which seems to have escaped the attention of historians.

When these preliminary proceedings had terminated successfully for the sheriff, he received his allowance, *not* on his original precept, but by a new writ tested at the Exchequer, thus fulfilling the words of the royal guarantee, 'and it shall be reckoned with you at the Exchequer.'

'The King, etc., to William of Faleise, etc. Find out of your farm that which shall be necessary by the view and testimony of the lawful men for making mews at Fereforde, and to repair the chimneys at Theok, and the windows, and it shall be reckoned with you at the Exchequer.
'Witness, myself at Winchester, the vij. day of May.'

When allowance had been thus made to the accountant, both the writs in question, original and official, were laid up in the marshal's county-bags. If, however, the transaction were incomplete, the sheriff was allowed *de tanto*, and permitted to keep the original for the time being, though the official writ was stored up.

Writs of allowance were, as a rule, of three kinds, namely, *Computate*, *Allocate*, and *Perdono* ; which purported to express the king's wishes, as communicated to the Barons, with respect to the case before them. All of them were addressed to the treasurer, or treasurer and Barons jointly, authorizing allowance or discharge to be respectively made, and were tested at the Exchequer formerly by two of the greater officials. In the later period dormant or permanent writs of *allocate*, etc., were often made out for an accountant, and kept on hand instead of being put aside on the conclusion of an isolated transaction. So,

too, partial writs of alleviation might be authorized by the crown for a debtor to have respite or
attermination of his account till the following
term, or even still later. These official writs
were all made out at the Exchequer by the
chancellor's scribe, who kept the receipts thereof
on behalf of the crown.

> 'The King, etc., to the Barons, etc. Place to the account
> of John de Builli, in his farm of Scarborough, that which he
> has expended in the necessary repair of our houses of Scar-
> borough, by the view and testimony of the lawful men,
> according to the custom of our Exchequer.
> 'Witness, etc.'

It was held to be essential that all origina
precepts should either express the amount of the
outlay authorized, or that the satisfaction of the
tenor of the precept should be proved on the part
of the accountant. In the same way all official
writs of allowance or discharge must absolutely
specify the sum allowed or discharged respectively.
Otherwise, the holder of them was not acquitted
at the Exchequer.

In case of the king's absence, the justiciar was
ex officio regent of the kingdom, and at such
times all writs, original or official, ran in his
name, and were then tested by him, and by the
treasurer and constable, for the two kinds respectively. As long, however, as the king was
in England, original writs ran in his name, and

were tested by him alone ; while official writs ran also in his name, but were tested by the justiciar and constable, or two other of the greater officials.

4. *The Trial of the Pyx.*

The lower chamber of the Exchequer of Receipt was managed by certain officials who were both subordinate and also subservient to the greater officers, that is, the Barons of the upper chamber, or Exchequer of state. Such were the treasurer's clerk, the two knights of the chamberlains, and the usher, who may be considered as the deputy of the marshal in the upper chamber. But besides these, the clerical officials of the staff, there were others employed as experts in connection with the necessary manipulation of the currency itself; to wit, a knight by rank—who may be called the master of the assays*—his working subordinate, the assayer, and four tellers.

The latter were solely occupied in counting the silver pennies poured into the treasury in *rouleaux* of £100, which were then placed in bags, sealed and labelled by the treasurer's clerk. The only test of the standard of the currency applied in this numeration was, first, to mix the coinage impartially, and then to weigh each counted pound separately, sixpence each librate being allowed as the limit for

* Literally, the ' knight-silverer.'

any deficiency in weight, under which standard no receipts were admitted by tale.

We have seen that in the earliest times—previously, that is, to the reorganization of the Exchequer under Henry I.—the revenue of the sovereign was answered in two forms, namely, in specie and in kind ; the former drawn from judicial fines and farms of towns, and the latter rendered, at an arbitrary assessment, by the cultivators of the royal demesne. The ever-increasing needs of the crown, however, together with the temptation for official exactions, which was offered by an arbitrary tallage in kind, caused the latter plan to be commuted for by an assessment, in specie alone, upon each of the king's farms in demesne. Then all of these, being at length consolidated into one farm for each county, were entrusted to the administration of a sheriff or custos, who answered for the same at the Exchequer, as well as for the judicial issues of his bailiwick.* At first this agent of the crown paid in the revenue of his county by tale, with the proviso added that he should make good

---

* Thus the simplest distinction primarily made between sheriffs, who rendered their accounts by tale or in blank, respectively, was by taking into consideration whether the issues of courts of justice, *i.e.*, of the hundred, etc., were consolidated with the farm of the county, or retained in the king's hand. In the former case the payment was in blank, in the latter by tale.

a presumed deficiency in weight on every counted pound by a vantage-payment of sixpence.   Later this modest compensation was found inadequate to protect the crown from loss through a depreciated standard of currency ; therefore, instead of making such a payment *ad scalam*, as the vantage-money system* was called, the sheriff was now required to account for the actual weight of every counted pound paid in by him—which was known as the payment *ad pensum*—or to compound with a shilling in the pound for vantage-money in lieu thereof.   Later still, when not only the weight, but even the fineness of the currency, had begun to suffer a depreciation, Roger, Bishop of Salisbury, the leading spirit of Henry I.'s financial innovations, introduced the further expedient of blanching the farms of the counties—that is to say, of requiring them to be paid either in tested bullion, or in specie which must be reduced to that condition before it was admitted at the Exchequer. This regulation was forthwith carried out, except in the case of a few counties, privileged chiefly on account of the non-existence or paucity of local moneyers.   Some time, however, naturally elapsed before the reform could be carried into universal effect.

* The payment *ad scalam* differed from that by tale, in that the former was subject in all cases to the deduction of sixpence on each librate.

Fig. 24.—Seal of Alphonso, of Castille.

Thus in the thirty-first year of Henry I. we find a dozen or so of the principal counties accounted for in blank, and about the same number by weight, with half that number by tale. Yet some, such as Lincoln and Warwick, are answered for both in blank and by weight ; others—to wit, Bucks and Beds—in blank and by tale ; others, again—for example, Kent—by weight and tale ; and one, Lincoln, by all three methods of account.

In the sixth year of Henry II., however, the system had become far more uniform in favour of payments in blank or, apparently, by its equivalent of scale, when no other arrangement was specified, which represented a uniform deduction of sixpence from every pound. In some few cases, however, as in that of Kent, the farm was answered both in blank and by tale.

Whenever it happened that the treasure paid into the Receipt fell below the standard of weight— which deficiency was established by weighing every heap of 1,200 pence in a wooden coffer, 30 pence being thrown in to turn the scale if necessary—or if it was paid in on account of a farm liable to be blanched, the following ceremony was performed : The master of assays, taking possession of a coffer containing 44 shillings worth of coin chosen at random out of the farm paid in by the sheriff, which coffer was first sealed with the latter's seal, carried it forthwith into the upper Exchequer, and emptied its contents on the table. Then, the coin being again mixed by hand, a pound's worth of the whole was carefully weighed against a pound weight of the realm in the Exchequer scale. This done, the librate was counted to ascertain whether it contained 240 pence. If the result of this scrutiny were satisfactory, the sheriff was next required to proceed to the assay, prepaying the assayer's fee of twopence out of his own pocket.

Besides the sheriff and the master of assays, with his subordinates, two other sheriffs, nominated by the treasurer, were present at the ceremony as witnesses. Together this party repaired to the furnace, whither the assayer had preceded them, to make the necessary preparations. Arrived there, the coffer containing the trial librate was once more emptied and counted afresh by the expert, the rest standing by watching his operations. When counted, the coins were thrown into the melting-pot, reduced to a liquid mass, and the dross skimmed by the assayer under the critical gaze of the officials and the sheriffs, each side keen to note, on behalf of its conflicting interests, whether the metal were, on the one hand, insufficiently purified, or, on the other, over-refined by the negligence of the melter. But, as a rule, the expert caught the pot from the charcoal at the exact juncture prescribed by the rules of his art, and emptied its contents into a vessel, which was then carried by the master of assays, accompanied by the rest of the party, before the Barons. If, however, the expert declared the assay to have failed, or if the experiment were challenged by either party, the whole ceremony was gone through again, with another librate out of the surplus store, the assayer, however, receiving no fresh fee in this case.

In the upper chamber of state the silver bullion resulting from the assay was weighed in the scale against the standard pound, and the loss by the fire made up by the sheriff throwing in sufficient pence out of the surplus in the pyx to turn the scale. Thereupon the refined librate was put aside, endorsed with the name of the county to which it appertained, together with a certificate of the number of pence which had been required to make up the loss by the assay, whereby it was established how many pence were to be deducted from every pound which the farm contained before it could be allowed as 'blanched'—a deduction amounting on an average to five *per cent.* on the whole sum paid in, whether in cash or tallies.

5. *Foreign Accounts.*

The great roll continued to be made up in the same form until the end of the reign of Henry III. Even in the earliest surviving specimens it can be seen that this formula involved much repetition, more especially in respect of individual debts of which there was little chance of payment.   These tedious repetitions have also proved a fruitful source of confusion to later students, as will be evident from the following instance : In the Pipe Roll of the fifth year of Henry II. there occurs, under the county of Cambridge, the entry, ' The sheriff renders account of 2 marks for Fugelmera.' The same entry recurs in most of the year rolls throughout this reign.   In the ninth year, however, one mark was paid off. Somewhat later another half-mark was paid, but the remainder was still charged as a forlorn hope till nearly the end of the reign, when the entry at last disappears. But the worst was this, that the scribe occasionally varied the monotony of the repeated entry by a change of form, which made it appear at one time as though it were a place under notice, at another as a person, and yet again as a local tax or custom, under all which heads it was indexed in turn. Some persons even thought that this was the name of a Saxon lady.   It is clear, however, that Foulmire, in Cambridgeshire, is meant, which escheated to the crown in 1158, with other possessions of Earl Conan of Brittany.

In the fifty-fourth year of Henry III. steps were taken to reform this troublesome procedure by means of a distinction between good and bad debts, and in the twelfth year of Edward I. a new method of entry was established, by which the sheriff's farms were to be entered in a separate roll (just as they were formerly set out in the great Exactory Roll under Henry II., no specimen of which is known to have survived), and the bad debts in the same way in another roll. Henceforth the sums mentioned therein were to be collected by the sheriff as he was best able, and were not to be entered in the great roll until they were paid. As, however, a large proportion of these bad debts was made up of 'dead farms,' both items came to be written in the same roll, which was called Exannual Roll.

But long before the date of this important innovation it had been found impossible to find space for the rapidly increasing casual revenue of the crown in the Pipe Roll itself. It had, indeed, from the first been usual to enter in the great roll only the total allowance demanded by an accountant for necessary or authorized disbursements, the details of his account being contained in a 'roll of particulars,' which was carefully preserved for further examination. In the same way the details of the sums collected by such revenue officers as Customers and others were also rendered separately in the form of ledgers or rolls of particulars, and the totals only were entered in the great roll. In course of time all the rapidly-increasing revenue derived from extraordinary sources, such as the Customs, were now accounted for in supplementary rolls, constituting, in fact, a separate return. These were called the foreign accounts, which comprised a great variety of subjects.

The summonses of the sheriffs were originally prepared by the chancellor's representative at the Exchequer, and all other processes for levying the king's debts also issued out of Chancery. When, therefore, the Chancery was separated from the Exchequer, at the end of the twelfth century, the custom arose of 'estreating,' or extracting, all notices of debts due to the king in respect of fines or grants, etc., entered on the Chancery rolls, which estreats were sent to the Exchequer in order that they might be levied from the debtors. These Chancery estreats were called *Originals*, and a long series of Originalia rolls still exists. In the earliest period the king's justices delivered into the Exchequer rolls or lists of the fines and amercia-ments levied by them in the king's courts, which may be regarded as a form of estreats, since they were evidently extracts from the formal records of that court. When the king's court, like the Chancery, became a distinct department from the Exchequer, these extracts were known as the foreign estreats in distinction to the originals received from the Chancery. It is a curious fact that this system of estreating has prevailed in most

Fig. 25.—Seal of the Golden Bull of Pope Clement VII.

of the administrative departments of the state for other than financial purposes, but with the same object—namely, to set the proper machinery in motion for the furtherance of the king's service ; that is to say, whenever distinct departments of the state have been created for special purposes, such as the Admiralty, War Office, Treasury, Foreign Office, Colonial Office, etc., extracts from all despatches, or intelligence, or accounts received by the Government have been transmitted to departments in order that the technical steps might be taken for appropriate action.

Towards the end of the reign of Edward I., the system of returning the extraordinary or casual revenue of the crown under a separate form of account was still further developed by the institution of the Greenwax. The origin of this name is found in the green wax used in the composition of the seal appended to the summonses which were now issued for payment of petty fines and amerciaments separately from the ordinary summonses to the sheriffs. The greenwax was under the supervision of the clerk of the estreats and of the king's Remembrancer, but in the reign of James I. a surveyor-general of the greenwax was appointed. It may be observed that this, like most other casual sources of revenue, was frequently oppressively enforced, and was highly unpopular.

Provision having thus been made for the collection of the extraordinary and casual revenue of the crown, no longer included in the great roll, further steps were taken for auditing the same before the foreign apposer, who here took the place of the Chancellor's clerk.   The result of this audit was entered in two separate rolls, one for those debts which were paid, the other for those which remained unpaid, according as the entries were ' totted ' or ' nichilled ' by the accountant.

CHAPTER VII.

THE MAKING OF THE BUDGET.

IT would probably be found a very difficult matter to compile a table of the revenue of this country, distinguishing between the several sources of income or profit enjoyed by the crown in the several historical periods embraced within the Anglo-Saxon, Norman, and Plantagenet dynasties. With the close of the Middle Ages, many of these sources had become dry, or else diverted from their proper channels, so that a revolution in financial practice was imminent, and was eventually accomplished at the expense of most of the mediæval theories which had survived the civil war of the middle of the seventeenth century; but many fictions lingered, almost to the beginning of the present reign, as was only natural when the administration of the national finances was carried on by the same machinery that had been in motion for over seven hundred years. It will be better, therefore, to avoid the common view of a separate system of

national finance for each of the above epochs,
more particularly in the case of the Anglo-Saxon
and Norman periods.   The following table may be
taken as fairly representative of the chief sources
of the national revenue during the greater part of
the Middle Ages, and the continuity of each of
these may be gathered from subsequent remarks:

I.—ORDINARY REVENUE.

(i.) Crown lands.
   (*a*) Royal farms.
   (*b*) Casual farms, such as woodrents, etc.
   (*c*) Lands in the king's hands by escheat,
        forfeiture, vacancy, etc.
   (*d*) Feefarms of towns and gilds, etc.

(ii.) Casual revenue, including coinage, tolls and
        markets, treasure-trove, wreck, royal
        fish, deodands, waifs and strays, goods
        of felons, usurers, fugitives, outlaws,
        recreants.

(iii.) Control of trade.
   (*a*) Purveyance or pre-emption.
   (*b*) Prisage.
   (*c*) Customs.

(iv.) Issues of justice.
   (*a*) Fines.
   (*b*) Amerciaments.

(v.) Feudal taxation.

    (*a*) Aids (the three accustomed).

    (*b*) Tallage.

    (*c*) Scutage.

    (*d*) Relief, marriage, wardship, etc.

II.—EXTRAORDINARY REVENUE.

(i.) Danegeld.

(ii.) Aid (imperial ; the *Donum*, etc.).

(iii.) Scutage and carucage or hidage (imperial).

(iv.) Subsidy on land.

(v.) Tenths and fifteenths (or other proportion).

(vi.) Subsidy on wools, etc

The story of the Teutonic migration relates that the victorious leader of an invading tribe divided the conquered territory between himself and his armed followers, leaving certain tracts, unsuited for immediate occupation by reason of their wooded or marshy nature, for the constitutional requirements of the embryo state.

From a very early date, the tendency had been for the crown to treat the public lands as its own, for purposes of the State at least. The sole check upon this pretension existed in the supposed consent of the Witan to every alienation of the property of the nation. Somewhat later it was found that this new claim of the crown was neither wholly interested, nor in itself disadvantageous to the national cause. The king was no longer a mere tribal leader, responsible, at most, for the regulation of his household, great and small. The national defence, the establishment of justice, the maintenance of law and order by a strict police to meet the immediate wants of a new-born civil society, or the prospective wants of a mercantile community, were now his care. The folklands of the ninth and tenth centuries, stripped of their fairer members by the appropriations or feudal grants of previous sovereigns, consisted mainly of forest, moor, and marsh, or those narrower tracts of soil, including highways and river-beds, which served as marshes or boundaries between sub-kingdoms, shires, and hundreds.

And so the change supposed to have been in progress since the Battle of Ellandune is known to have been accomplished before the Conquest by the evidence of *Domesday Book*. Here we find the crown actually in possession of the ancient folkland, which passes under the generic title of *Terra Regis*. There is not much evidence to show to what extent the latter benefitted by this appropriation ; and there is none to show when or how it took place. We have merely, then, to accept *Terra Regis* of *Domesday* as we find it, and to follow the constitutional interest connected with its enlargement or decrease during subsequent reigns. At first we are presented with a steady increase. The royal demesne of the Conqueror must have been a large one, judging from the entries thereof in *Domesday Book*, and the popular impression expressed by the chroniclers ; and this territory was steadily increased by his sons, especially in the direction of afforestation. For this latter encroachment we should have been prepared from our knowledge of the domestic policy of Norman kings, who undertook the administration of national resources for ensuring law and order in return for a territorial enjoyment and profit becoming more and more invidious and absolute, and a territorial jurisdiction verging upon tyranny, even as it is seen under the milder rule of the first Plantagenet. However, these things are as yet known to us mostly by capable conjecture.

The next piece of direct evidence which follows Domesday is the surviving Pipe Roll of Henry I. Here we find plentiful mention of crown lands granted, sold, or given in exchange to vassals and officials. In the Pipe Rolls of Henry II., which succeed this isolated record, instances of such grants are found in still greater abundance, and made like the former to officials of the new school created by Henry I., rather than on the principle of feudal concession which characterized the alienations of a weak king like Stephen, and unpatriotic

rulers like Henry III., Edward II., Richard II.,
and Henry VI.

Although the tenants of folk-land under state
control formed a body of vassals ready made at
the period of the extension of the royal jurisdiction
over the ancient property of the nation, and paying, in the case of towns, at least, very substantial
rents in the shape of 'Gable' money, it is probable
that, previous to the reign of Henry I., the purely
agricultural rents of the crown lands were mostly
paid in kind, and that this inconvenient practice
was only abandoned after an agitation which
threatened, at one time, to become a prædial
war.

Richard Fitz-Nigel, treasurer of King Henry
II., gives, in his famous treatise on the Exchequer,
the following graphic account of this financial
revolution :

'In order that you may comprehend these things,
it is necessary to go back a little further.   According to tradition of the time of our fathers, in the
primitive state of the kingdom following the Conquest, the kings received payment for their farms
not in weight of gold or silver, but in victuals
alone, out of which those things that were
necessary for the daily consumption of the king's
house used to be provided.   And they knew—
they who were appointed for this purpose—how
much was forthcoming from every farm.   For the

rest, to defray the pay or largesse of the soldiers, and other necessities, coined money was provided from the pleas and conventions of the crown, and from the cities or castles which did not practise agriculture. Therefore, during the whole reign of King William I., and down to the time of King Henry, his son, this practice prevailed, so that I myself have encountered those who have seen victuals conveyed to the court, at the times appointed, from the royal farms, the officers of the king's house being exactly informed from which counties wheat, and from which the several kinds of flesh, or the provender for horses, or the other necessaries, were owing. Then, on payment being made of these things, in manner appointed, the royal officers entered them to the credit of the sheriff, reducing their value into money—namely, for a measure of wheat sufficient for the bread of a hundred men, one shilling ; for the carcass of a grazing ox, one shilling ; for a ram or sheep, four-pence ; for the provender of twenty horses, like-wise fourpence. But in a subsequent period, when this same king was engaged in foreign and distant parts in suppressing the tumults of war, it became desirable for him to have the requisite sum for these exploits in coined money. Meanwhile, a clamorous throng of countrymen had flocked to the king's court, or, which he took more griev-ously, even threw themselves in his way on his progresses, bringing in their ploughshares as a token of the decay of agriculture ; for they were oppressed by hardships unnumbered by reason of the victuals which they used to convey from their own abodes throughout divers parts of the realm. Therefore, the king, giving ear to their complaints, by the deliberate counsel of his great men, despatched throughout the kingdom those whom he knew to be most prudent and discreet for that purpose, who, passing round and surveying each farm, by the evidence of their own eyes, an estimate being taken of the victuals that were payable therefrom, reduced the amount to a money sum. But for the total sum which arose from all the farms in one county, they appointed the sheriff of that county to be answerable at the Exchequer.'*

The same author tells us in another place that he had also conversed with old men who had witnessed the vast herds of cattle and the heavily-laden wains with which every road was choked in the environs of the court on the eve of a great festival or foreign expedition.

It is probable that the crown lands, like the French possessions of this country, reached their greatest extent in the reign of Henry II. From this point, therefore, we are engaged in noting their steady decline, in spite of certain arbitrary,

* *Dialogus,* i. 7.

even desperate, attempts to expiate the evils of voluntary or forced alienations.

From the very first we have seen that the acquirement of an extensive royal demesne by the crown was, in fact, the result of an indirect bargain with the nation. The king took over the residue of the folk-land, because he alone was qualified by the possession of an equivalent territorial jurisdiction to undertake their management and order. So, too, with regard to the later revenue which the crown derived, directly or indirectly, from the soil, it had come to be regarded as an essential condition of its enjoyment that the king should ' live of his own '; he for his part undertaking the defence of the national independence, commerce, and interests of every kind, from harmful influences, particularly such as were brought about by the growing competition of other countries — in fact, such a programme as is described in the words of Edward I., ' ut terra de bonis suis se illæsa conservaret.' Now, one of the most baneful of these influences was favouritism, or countenancing aliens. This anti-English policy was truly the curse of Plantagenet kings. John and Henry III. used it ; so did Edward II., Edward III., Richard II., and Henry VI. Opposition to this new freak of the crown is the chief explanation of popular discontent on many notable occasions, and is easily identified as the mainspring of the national policy formulated in 1258, 1297, 1312, 1340, and 1386. That is to say, the royal demesne, under all the kings above mentioned, was wantonly alienated for the benefit of favourites, and these the vilest men in the popular view. Stephen had already set an example which had been deprecated by the thrift of his successor, but all too readily followed out for a still worse motive by Richard I. and John. Thanks to a long and profitable minority, Henry III. began his personal government with sufficient resources for a constitutional programme ; but in his reign we have not only the most aggravated instances of wasteful grants of royal property (now, since Magna Carta, regarded as the property of the nation, when the nation might no longer be arbitrarily taxed in default), but the fatal expedient of forced resumptions—the bankrupt monarch's discharge through the good graces of ministers or Parliament.

Of the remaining branches of the crown lands, woodrents and other casual profits of the old waste folk-lands were not, from the evidence of the Pipe Rolls at least, of any special value during this early period. The case was very different, however, from the close of the fourteenth century onwards, though there is reason to believe that this portion of the revenue was very indifferently administered by its local officers.

The case of the baronies or manors which fell into the hands of the crown by way of escheat or forfeiture was widely different. It is not too much to assert that from first to last few estates of importance escaped the consequences of the feudal doctrine of survivorship, and it would be probably impossible to form any approximate estimate of the increase of revenue which might have accrued to the crown from this one source. Unfortunately for themselves and their heavily-taxed subjects, the later Plantagenet kings notoriously neglected their opportunities of absorbing overgrown peerages, for by a strange fatality those opportunities most frequently arose during the reigns of weak and improvident sovereigns. Even so the rent-roll of honours, bishoprics, or towns 'in the king's hand' during the latter part of the twelfth and the whole of the thirteenth century was very considerable. As regards the remaining source of revenue under this head, namely, that derived from the farms of towns and gilds, it may be said that it formed a welcome, though by no means ample, contribution to the royal treasury. Some cities, such as London, paid their farms regularly down to recent times, but others were compelled to seek relief on the grounds of natural decay, or at one time of damage from a foreign invasion.

The casual revenue of the crown was a still

more uncertain source of wealth. It was a point of honour with a bold peasantry to simplify the process of collecting treasure-trove or wreck of the sea or waifs by leaving nothing to be collected. Royal fish (whale, etc.), indeed, was readily presented, probably because it was unpalatable without the resources of the royal kitchen ; and deodands, which were regarded with superstitious abhorrence, being worth, moreover, some few pence only in most cases, were promptly rendered to the crown. The monopoly of coinage probably paid the working expenses of the Mint, while the more valuable estrays were for the most part conceded by the crown itself to local lords. Certainly long lists of felons' goods, etc., appear in several of the Pipe Rolls of the period ; but the sums accounted for were both trivial and with difficulty collected, though the goods of usurers, whether Jews or Christians, were at times very valuable acquisitions.

The revenue of the crown from its control of trade was probably the most considerable of any except the actual farms of the crown lands.

In the primitive idea of Teutonic kingship, the possession of an imperial revenue, it is needless to insist, is never entertained. The princeps, or dux, attended by his following of elders or warriors, has an instrument ever ready to his hand for defensive or offensive action. Whether he be a descendant of the demigods, or the hero of a momentous crisis, it is equally obvious to his followers that, as the leader of their choice, he must receive something more than moral support at their hands. His is no paternal government which, backed by an ample Exchequer, can train and feed men for home or foreign warfare. It rests on nothing more than the influence of personal prestige, and, from a worldly point of view, their ruler is no better than *primus inter pares.* But this penniless champion is one, they feel (the history of their race is an oft-taught lesson to them), who can lead them from victory to victory, direct them to booty upon booty; who can promote them from a province to a kingdom, and exalt them from a clan into a nation. The tribesman, therefore, fights both for himself and his chief; he for success and the glory which it brings. The former provides the materials for the enterprise—service at his own expense, and contributions in kind to maintain the rude splendour of his patron's state. The latter stakes the honour of his family upon the results of his own wisdom and prowess. The fight is won. The chief becomes king, his tribe a kingdom. He becomes also a great landlord, with tracts of conquered territory at his disposal. These he distributes amongst his retainers, whose personal attachment, now exchanged for a feudal obligation, is in no way lessened by their altered circumstances, but strengthened and multiplied infinitely by the possession of individual power and patronage. The king is now no longer a simple patriarch, but a dread liege, a sovereign by Divine right and human force. He is rich above his vassals ; can play the potentate, or the patron, at his good pleasure. But with power comes either the sense of its insecurity, or the fresh lust of conquest.

For now the kingdom is pitted against rival kingdoms ; the onslaught grows to an invasion ; the battle is lengthened into a campaign. The direction of the ruler becomes more necessary, his requirements more pressing. He must have more steeds, more panoplies, more sheep and oxen at his disposal. At last, he or his successors lead their host to a crowning victory. Rival dynasties are overthrown ; scattered sub-kingdoms are amalgamated. The victor finds himself upon the throne of a great nation. Then at length his kingship begins to assert itself. He is not only the leader of his people in war, but their administrator in peace. He is the supreme landlord, the origin of justice, the patentee of heaven for honours and privileges and emoluments which he alone of all others can aspire to ; and this is his prerogative—this distinguishes him from all the rest, and is his guarantee for that supremacy which is needful to the trust which has been imposed upon him, the well-being of his subjects.

The latter have dispersed to take possession of their lots, to map out, to build, and cultivate the soil. Their great men remain a caste of vigilant and restless warriors. The humbler sort become a native peasantry, or turn their enterprise to the pursuit of trade. The one great obligation of self-defence is still upon them all. Each man must hold himself ready, at his lord's call, in his person, and with his labour and substance, in the king's wars. With the latter there is no distinction between public and private emergencies. What he sacrifices for the general good he equally dispenses for his own personal advantage. He represents the unity of the race, and his action is only magnified in theirs. A danger is at hand, and the nation must repel it at whatever cost. Granting its existence, what that danger is, or how or whence, is for the moment at least no affair of theirs. Such is the position that they have accepted by adopting a system which alone has wrought their greatness.

Suppose, then, that an army of defence has voluntarily assembled, equipped, and even provisioned, for a certain space of time at individual expense. But, except under the most primitive conditions of warfare, a still greater outlay will be needed to keep it under arms, to brace the sluggish mass with the sinews of war. Whence are these funds to be procured? From the first it was decided that all must contribute where the safety of all was concerned. But now all are not fit to bear arms ; moreover, all are not now accessible. The nation has shifted the responsibility of its defence upon the king. He has resources of his own, a revenue, such as it is, sufficient for the expenses of state. The quarrel is his ; let him bear the brunt himself. That is what actually came to pass, as, indeed, was inevitable in a state pretending to civilization. In this aspect the king was the state, and, it may be added, always has been. The tribal warrior did not load his chief with arms and necessaries for the latter's private aggrandizement, but to qualify him for his post as champion of the race ; 'to do him honour,' we are told, 'and also to relieve his necessities.'* Now, this honour was essentially for the credit of the community, and the necessity of the hour was equally a concern of their own.

Thus we find that in the latter period to which we were referring, the new nation endowed their king with a prerogative derived apparently from that early system of oblations of levying supplies at discretion to meet his sovereign requirements ; in other words, the right of prisage, pre-emption, or purveyance. The personal security or pre-eminence of the ruler before the world was, in those days, and for long after, the first object of

* Tacitus, 'Germania,' c. xiv.

statecraft. Next to this his dignity and state were of the most importance. Therefore, above all things, he must be a victorious ruler; and he must also be strong in justice and conspicuous in splendour. He was paid to be efficient; but he was not left to regulate the pay according to the efficiency displayed. No such principle is even yet consistently recognised; but at this point the ruler is left to his own devices. Those are various; some creditable, others the reverse. Here it concerns us only to trace the constitutional origin and scope of one of them.

The king had, in Anglo-Saxon times, we may believe, the prerogative of prisage or purveyance— the admitted right to purchase, 'for his own use,' stores or material at an official discretion with regard to quantity or price. He represented the glory of the nation, and his equipage, appointments, and hospitality, must be such as to magnify the post. Of what did this executive task consist? If we reduced the expenditure incurred therein to an average, it would be found to be two-thirds for fighting, and the residue for dress and diet. Therefore, for every charger or harness which the crown required in the public service to grace some pomp or ceremony, for every ox slaughtered for the royal table, twice as many again would figure in the field of war, or replenish the salting-tubs of a royal garrison.

Roughly speaking, the supplies of which the king stood in need were of two kinds : (1) Provisions for his household and retinue for everyday consumption ; for feast-days and ceremonies ; for journeys and expeditions at home and abroad. (2) Dress and appointments for the same on like occasions.

For three centuries after the Conquest there was no limit finally established for the demand thus created. If the king and his men were 'at home' on any working day of the year, a comparatively modest supply was sufficient for the requirements of the royal household. On any festival day, and especially those on which the king wore his crown, according to custom, preparations on a much larger scale were necessary. During a campaign or state progress abroad, the ordinary arrangements of the service underwent a complete change. The court was now a camp, the retinue an army. There were 10,000 mouths to feed instead of 1,000, and a like increment in the expenditure requisite for their equipment. It is true that under the Norman kings this excrescence was not readily perceptible. The vassal followed his lord at his own cost. The executive had no responsibility as to whether or no the militiaman starved in that service, and therefore it often happened that the men of his county supplied him with funds sufficient for his support during the campaign. With the Plantagenet kings came the great change in feudal warfare—the commutation of personal service for an assessment in money or kind. Henceforth for the most part the sovereign waged war at his own expense, defrayed by the existing revenues of the crown. The necessary supplies for the palace or the castle-camp, the hunting excursion or the foreign progress, for each and for all, were levied by the king's mandate from his subject producers. The process was as follows : The crown required oxen and sheep and corn for the royal household or army—'ad opus nostrum et nostrorum.' Then a writ of privy seal was directed to its officers in the counties— the sheriffs in most cases—commanding such provision to be made at the royal expense, for the officer was allowed the nominal outlay incurred in his account. If wine were lacking for a like service, the king's chamberlains at London and Sandwich, in early times, took from each cargo landed in England, unfranked, one cask on each side of the mast, at the most, for half its market value. If this were not enough to furnish the quota specified, part of the cargo was purchased at a slightly higher rate. It even happened, by no means unfrequently, too, that a ship, with all its cargo of wine, was chartered by the crown, and navigated forthwith to the required point ; but it seems to have been usual to subject only foreign vessels to this exaction. In like manner clothing,

arms, horses, and miscellaneous stores were procured indiscriminately for the royal need or gratifi-
cation. ' Ad opus regis et suorum ' was a password
that opened every grange or warehouse.

In the age of which we are speaking the king
had not only the prescriptive right to obtain relief
for the necessities of his person or of his state from
the products of the soil—lead, iron, tin, corn,
cattle, wool, and even articles of staple manufacture—but he also acquired by means hereof a
species of vested interest in the prevailing distribution of those forms of wealth. In one aspect,
as the supreme landlord of the nation, he was im-
plicated in his tenants' welfare. Their prosperity
was the security for the strength and efficiency of
his rule, and he felt justified in insisting that the
security should be tangible. It is thus that we
arrive at the explanation of the fact that the
crown, in the earliest period of our history, had
the absolute regulation of internal traffic, of sale
or barter between its subjects, in its own hands.
If a tenant's wealth, by his own simplicity or
negligence, became diverted into other channels,
this event, the economic importance of which was
so slight, was otherwise disastrous to the crown.
It had lost the efficient service of a fighting man,
and it had also lost an available contribution to
its own possible necessities. The spirit which
prompted the enactments preventing a freeman

from parting with his arms under any circumstances was the same with that which ordered the form of his bargains with his neighbours, and debarred him from the risks and profits alike of international commerce. It is proper to insist much upon this explanation of the undoubted phenomenon of the crown alone possessing the right to erect a market at large for the produce of the land. Historians are apt to dwell upon the necessity ever present to the chief magistrate, of keeping the peace between his turbulent subjects, as a readier solution of the problem ; and in one sense the suggestion is a reasonable one. It was, indeed, essential that each party to the primitive bargains of the period should be convinced that the other had a ' clean-back,' as their jargon went ; but this theory will not explain the still wider control of the crown for the commercial welfare of the nation at large, exercised without question into far later times. In any case, the fact remains that under no circumstances was a subject of this kingdom at liberty to absent himself beyond the cognizance of the Government, even in the pursuit of his lawful occupation. Neither might such a one export or transport to a distant place any commodity of the kingdom without the royal license. Thus, he could not at his own will consign a cargo of tin, wood, wool, leather, corn, flesh, fish, or other staple articles to the order of a

Flemish agent, or of a fellow-subject in one of the French dependencies of the English erown. Nay, more! It was an admitted fact that the sovereign's prerogative was infringed, his state impaired, by any such transaction, and amends must be made on either score by the payment of a substantial fine in consideration of a royal license to trade in the way proposed. In the face of this fundamental right, how are we to dismiss the notion of the crown's proprietary interests in the products of the soil from our minds? It would seem as though the sovereign, holding that the entire native wealth of the kingdom lay at his disposal for the relief of those needs which were incurred by his royal state or responsibilities, would suffer no portion thereof to be removed beyond his reach without compensating his revenue for the possible losses which it might thus sustain.

It is far less probable that the crown, in its infinite wisdom and justice and strength, should have immediately arrived at the following compact with its subjects in their interests, which the orthodox sticklers for an illimitable constitution have loved to suppose : that it should, with the consent of all, have been allowed to levy definite contributions from merchandise which passed through the outports to maintain the safety of the seas ; from the inland carts and barges to maintain the king's peace upon the highways and common rivers ; and at the gates and quays of its great cities to ensure the latter a decent provision for an orderly municipal government, or for a strong imperial occupation in the interests of its own state and revenue.

It is true, however, that the latter object did seemingly enter into the calculations of the Government, and that the consideration which it received from its subjects on such occasions was in view of a twofold concession made to them on its own part. Those who fined to the crown for a license to traffic within the limits of its sovereign control were not only acquitted of all claims to ordinary prisage or toll, but received, at the same time, a guarantee for the safety of themselves and their property against any hindrance, seizure, or exaction whatsoever. Safety to whom and from what ? we should ask. The question is not a needless one, as we shall presently see.

The king's peace, except in the case of certain remote franchises, reigned throughout the length and breadth of the land. By a wise disposition, too, the authority of the crown was nowhere so jealously guarded, or so frequently exerted, as in the very spots where the maintenance of peace and order was most liable to be threatened. The waggoner or packhorse-driver and his master reflected as they plunged into the depth of a royal forest that, thanks to their sovereign's hobby in the shape of venery, not an outlaw dare make himself known in a country where the very highroads were beset with footpads, and paid their modest toll accordingly with willing hearts at the forest-gate. So, too, the wool-barge or hay-lighter which navigated the upper waters of the Thames gladly submitted to the *avalage* imposed by the king's bailiff or farmer. It could scarcely otherwise have been a pleasant passage for the market-boat of the reign of John within the clutches of such governors as might be in lack of stores in any royal castle from Windsor to Oxford. But even the hardiest of public robbers had a wholesome dread of poaching on royal preserves, lest he should be invited by the Exchequer Barons to fine for his acquittal in thirty marks, or should receive the royal missive at sight, of which he must surrender his command to the bearer. But all men who were not out of the pale of the law were entitled to the benefit of the king's peace, and certainly no exception was made to the disadvantage of the mercantile community.

Why, then, did the latter show themselves so desirous of obtaining the king's letters patent? The fact is that they were divided into two classes, each trading under different circumstances. The one was composed of native merchants, natural-born subjects—*indigenæ*, as they were called—who fined to the crown for license to export produce of the kingdom to a foreign mart; or only to transport it along the coast to one of the great English fairs, such as Boston or Lenn (Lynn). The other comprised foreign merchants, aliens, strangers, or *alienigenæ*, who equally fined for liberty to introduce themselves or their wares into England, subject to existing regulations. The former class received the king's protection from molestation, not at the hands of their fellow-countrymen, for the safeguard would have been needless, but to pass them safely through the officious hands of the royal Customers and bailiffs, who would otherwise have made short work of their liberty and cargoes by handing over the 'pirate' to the custody of the sheriff to await examination and heavy fine or bail in the Exchequer chamber, and by seizing and disposing of his merchandise as forfeit to the crown. The alien, on the other hand, did really stand in need of a safe-conduct, in view both of these official severities and still more of the jealous hatred of their own hopeful Customers, the en-lightened and protectionist natives of the land; for to the *custos* at the outport, the river-side baron, the wayside outlaw, and the town apprentice, the Lombard or Flemish pedlar, appeared fair game for violence and extortion in every form.

We have thus seen that the *custuma*, or practice of the crown to levy a revenue from produce exported from or imported into the kingdom, was a gradual development of the earlier *consuetudo*, or prerogative (for it was not from the first limited by the constitution, as some have supposed, but was the birthright of the sovereign from time immemorial), by virtue of which the king took prises of provisions or stuff to supply the exigencies of the state or warfare from his own subjects ; and exacted the same with a still higher hand from foreign traders, who might be both 'strangers' and 'foes,' according to the caprice of all rude nations. The one was a caption in peace, the other a capture of war, as the very etymology of the word suffices to prove, interpreted as it has been by the prescriptive usage of four whole centuries of recorded history. We shall now, therefore, be able to follow with a clearer understanding the following outline of the process which is found existent in very early times.

It would seem as though the first traces of the system of collecting a certain or uncertain toll from commodities of the land, or from foreign imports, were connected with the office of chamberlain of the king's household, or chamberlain of the cities of London and Sandwich. With regard to this appointment, it is important to note that the office of chamberlain was in immediate contact with the department of the king's wardrobe, which department had the administration of all that revenue (amongst others) which accrued from the royal prerogative of prisage in every form, and which (with the rest) was chiefly spent upon the pay of retainers or troops, and the supply of household provisions or munitions of war.

The remaining class of the Customs-revenue mentioned in these early records is that of a percentage on general merchandise in part acquittance, at least, of the old liability to prisage. The crown had quickly made the discovery that a permanent revenue was more easily raised from personal property than from real estate, and of the latter in the shape of a toll prepaid in hard cash, rather than of a more or less vexatious tithe in kind. Naturally the produce formally selected as the subject of this organized taxation was that which chiefly represented the superfluous wealth of the country, exported to foreign countries in payment of such necessaries or luxuries as were required for home consumption. From very early times this staple export was recognised as consisting of wool, woolfells, and leather. Wool, then, and hides were probably the chief source of Customs-revenue to the crown at the time when it was also in receipt of frequent fines for license to export less tangible articles of commerce.

Minerals, corn, cattle, and other produce did not offer such facilities for traffic or taxation on a twofold ground. In the first place, it was not easy to ensure in a rude and unquiet age more than a limited food-supply for the demands of the population ; neither was it expedient, on political grounds, to risk denuding the latter of the necessaries of life in order to furnish forth possible foes across the narrow seas. In the second place, the difficulties of rating products of this kind were admittedly great. In fact, until the problem was partially solved by the institution of a poundage on their intrinsic value only, such exports could not have contributed largely to the revenue collected from merchants by means of a disme or quinzime. In the thirteenth century we find the one-tenth, or other dividend, chiefly employed in the assessment of a constitutional taxation of property, the customary toll being fixed as a rateage on the bulk of staple exports. This was now practically reduced to the duty of 6s. 8d. upon every sack of wool, or its equivalent in 300 fells, and 13s. 4d. upon each last of hides exported. All other exports were either insignificant in amount, or were discouraged, and indeed, for the most part, wholly forbidden by the crown for motives of interest and policy. But when permitted, such exports paid Custom rather by a fine to the crown, or by suffering a heavy liability to prise, than by a fixed tariff.

In the case of imports whose existence was irksome to the patriotism as well as to the self-seeking spirit of the times, though the necessity for their toleration could not be denied, no scale of charge on the same plan as that of the ancient or great Customs of wools and leather was in force previous to the beginning of the fourteenth century. There was, it is true, a very ancient prerogative of the crown, limited by common law, though never by statute, for taking one cask out of ten, and two out of twenty—one, that is, on each side of the mast, from every cargo of imported wines ; but all other imports were, even more than uncustomed produce, liable to prisage at the mere discretion of the crown. In 1275 the rate of the older Custom upon exports was fixed by statute ; and in 1303 the convention of the crown, with alien merchants embodied in the Carta Mercatoria, settled the rates chargeable upon the imported wares of the latter.

These two enactments are the great landmarks in the history of our Customs-revenue, and with these that history properly commences. Meanwhile, neither such exports as were not included in the Statute of Westminster, nor any imports of native merchants, were subject to any fixed toll whatever, but continued to lie within the crown's prerogative of prisage. In spite of every opposition on the part of its subjects, that prerogative was exercised by successive sovereigns in what they took to be the kingdom's interests for centuries before it became forcibly disused.

It is probable that long before the absorption of the old folk-land into the royal demesnes it had already threatened to become a source of danger to the community. This was owing to its physical character as a region of pathless forests and wastes, the refuge of beasts of prey and of the chase ; the refuge also of still more dangerous marauders, outlaws and robbers, who subsisted upon the spoils less of nature than of the industry of man. Again, the highways and the great rivers, which presumably had been parcel of the public lands, were not only a source of anxiety in the matter of repairs and conservancy respectively, but were a positive inducement to crime. Three centuries later we find the crown still struggling with the evil, clearing the woods from the roadsides that no lurking-place might be afforded to highwaymen, and arming the rural population in its own defence against the daily commission of robberies and murders.

The folk-lands appear to have become crown-lands somewhere about the end of the ninth century, in exchange for which not very solid concession the sovereign was required to enter into that constitutional contract with his subjects which runs through our history as an expansion of the Anglo-Saxon coronation oath, which guaranteed the liberties of all in matters of religion, laws and justice.

Now, it was essential that the laws herein referred to should be 'good laws.' Furthermore, the Anglo-Saxon ideal of beneficent legislation was expressed in the traditional ordinances of Edward the Confessor, made with the approval of his wise men ; and in these enactments it will be observed that the theory of the king's responsibility for the preservation of the peace is strongly expressed, this peace being especially enjoined for the safety of all highways and great rivers. We may assume, then, that the vills, farms, forests, wastes, and highways before mentioned, as forming the physical structure of the folk-lands, were transferred to the crown as their natural custodian by the name of royal demesne in trust for the natural rights of the subject, together with an absolute jurisdiction, formulated at a later date as forest-law, conservancy and 'defence' of rivers and other highways, and a more than feudal proprietorship of vills and farms.

The profits of this new undertaking were naturally a considerable inducement. There were not only the farms cultivated or leased by the crown, and the produce whereof, at this early date, was rendered in kind by the farmers and bailiffs, and the 'Gable' rents above mentioned, but also there was the infinite vista of sport opened up to the Saxon monarch, who loved the chase within the forest glades of most southern shires. Moreover, there was the ample reward of a vigilant preservation of the peace upon the avenues of commerce in the shape of tolls and fines, paid willingly enough by the merchant in requital of this supreme safe-conduct, which passed him and his wares unharmed through the length and breadth of the land. Lastly, the crown was enriched by the net receipts from fines and amerciaments, the facilities for enforcing which were equally connected with this new jurisdiction over the former harbourage of crime.

In another aspect the peace of the Church must be considered in connection with the civil government of the temporal ruler. Here the Churchman appears as the skilled coadjutor of the rude tribal leader, devising modifications of spiritual privileges to meet the practical requirements of the lay subjects. In the bulk of Saxon laws and customs there is no idea more prominent than that of a bond between Church and State to ensure the preservation of peace, which was the first essential of moral and physical well-being. The king and the archbishop supported one another's dignity by a primitive law of treason and sacrilege, and the lives and property of their subjects and congregations by a penal code and ecclesiastical ordinances framed to cover every interest worthy of protection ; while the earl and the bishop sat together in the local courts to expound ' as well the law of

God as the secular law,' and to administer a prompt, yet pious, justice with the common assent and assistance of the great body of Christian freemen.

The progress of this idea may be traced in the legislative memorials of Anglo-Saxon nations ; or, perhaps, to be more accurate in the retrospective classification of English law, by Norman experts, until the highest point has been reached in the pretensions of the kingly state.

The following is the summary of the king's claim to be regarded as the 'fountain of justice':

'These are the prerogatives which the King of England alone and above all men enjoys for the preservation of peace and security: Breach of the peace bestowed by his hand, contempt of his writs or precepts, death or injury of his servants, infidelity and treason, disrespect of his person, fortifications without license, false coinage, outlawry, murder, robbery, burglary, assault with premeditation, narrowing highways, wreck, treasure-trove, forests, feudal incidents, Danegeld, fugitives from justice or battle, false judgments, perversion of laws, Churchmen, strangers, poor, needy, and friendless men,' etc.

Such is the fair growth of the king's peace from the germ of a patriarchal obligation tended by the devotion of the Church to the overshadowing expanse of a feudal prerogative trained by the civil lawyers. But, in spite of the insignificance of these feudal changes, they must still be regarded as the secular means which were justified by a spiritual end, rather than as a policy of mere self-seeking. This old simplicity of purpose is best seen in the coronation oaths and charters or other manifestoes of later Saxon, Norman, and Plantagenet sovereigns.

It was not long, however, before the purity of this patriarchal policy was sullied by the imputation of interested motives. Henceforth the king's peace was destined to become but another fiction of the constitution. The sovereign was no longer the leader, Rex Anglorum, the earlier Dux on an imperial scale, but the feudal proprietor, Rex Angliæ. The customary contributions of his subjects had become assessed by Domesday Survey, and commuted by scutage and carucage as forced taxes, grudgingly rendered and scornfully accepted as a scanty provision for the now extensive schemes of the European potentate. To supplement this meagre supply, the crown was now prepared to coin all its old benevolent prerogative into hard cash to meet the occasions of foreign war or household pomp, and an unfailing mine of wealth was opened in the dispensation of that protection which was now so necessary to its industrial subjects.

The simplest and commonest form of the king's protection was given under his hand, or, rather, seal, to the subject petitioner. This was the convenient charter which answered widely different purposes under the new régime of inquisitorial officialism that flourished after the Conquest, serving alike as a title-deed and an exemption from vexations, exactions, or litigation to those who could pay for its possession. This selfish policy was unfortunately facilitated by the administrative machinery devised by the first Plantagenet king, for the mere purpose, it seems, of being abused by his degenerate successors. An official traffic was carried on in charters, fines, and oblations, regularly entered to the credit side of a now exorbitant revenue.

The revenue derived from the issues of justice is usually classified under the two heads of fines and amerciaments, in which form they figure largely in the Exchequer records of the twelfth and thirteenth centuries. A fine, as is well known, was a fee taken by the crown in return for the employment of its good offices on behalf of applicants for offices, suitors for justice, or subjects distressed by some untoward event. In form, they were usually voluntary offerings to obtain the goodwill of the sovereign, and they might be tendered on occasion in kind as well as in money. Moreover, there was this implied bargain between the parties, that the fine could not be exacted until the consideration had been realized. In certain

desperate cases the crown lent its assistance only
in return for a large percentage of the desired
concession. The greater part of these fines fall
under the head of law-proceedings—namely, to
procure the king's writ for the expedition of a
suit, or to have respite from sentence pronounced,
or even ' for absolute pardon or release.'   In course
of time, however, the most valuable portion of
this revenue was derived from fines for protection
or license in respect of trade, and for commercial
or agricultural advantages interdicted by law.   All
of these when entered in the Chancery were returned to the Exchequer in due course to be
levied, or were estreated thither in the returns of
the king's justices.

   Amerciaments were derived from the pecuniary
mulcts imposed on offenders before the king's
justices.   Those who were convicted here were
supposed to lie at the king's mercy in respect of
their possessions, the penalty assessed being eventually the amerciament.   The offences which figure
most commonly in the Exchequer records are in
respect of trespasses of various kinds, defaults,
false claims or judgments, contempts, etc.   There
was also the famous murder fine imposed by the
Conqueror on the hundred in which a presumably
political murder had taken place.   The rate for
this alone is stated in the *Dialogus* to have been
£44, but it has been conclusively shown that a far

Fig. 26.—Seal of Francis I   (See p. 61.)

smaller rate actually prevailed.* The feudal income of the sovereign was not only made up from the royal demesnes, which were at the outset an allodial, and eventually a purely feudal possession, but more especially from the returns due from those portions which he had granted out to his feudal followers in respect of military service, or its equivalent money-value and certain recognised claims and liabilities respectively, which are usually known as feudal incidents. The nature of all of these is too well known to need any further explanation here. It will be enough to observe that this portion of the royal revenue was for the greater part of the thirteenth century in a transition state between a normal tax and an imperial levy as far as those items known as scutage and aid were concerned.

From the earliest times the king's personal income had constituted the chief pecuniary resource of the Government, though it would not be correct to say that the national resources were entirely at the king's disposal, because the application of this revenue from first to last has been controlled, in however slight a degree, by the counsel and consent of the subjects. In theory truly the king was then, and for centuries afterwards, the only authorized power for the collection of the revenue and for its administration. More-

* *Dialogus,* i. 10, discussed in Pike's 'History of Crime.'

over, a considerable part of the revenue was derived from the exercise of his mere prerogative. But although the sovereign was in theory the absolute owner of the land and the fountain of justice and honours alike, the profits which accrued to him from these sources were barely sufficient in any period to enable him 'to live of his own,' and do not seem to have excited the jealousy of the peers or the discontent of the commons. It was the same with the remaining sources of his income, the casual and feudal revenue. The king was the natural recipient of such windfalls as treasure-trove and the wreck of the sea, and this branch of the revenue has survived unquestioned down to our own times. Neither could it be gainsaid that the king, having established his title to the surplus land of the nation at the Conquest, had a right to expect some reasonable equivalent for military grants in the shape of military service and its correlative incidents. It was only when the crown abused its sacred trust that the necessity for drawing a sharp distinction between the ordinary and extraordinary revenue arose, the one henceforth a permissive enjoyment within certain limitations in respect of the larger items of purveyance, the Customs and fines of justice, and the other entirely subject to the control of Parliament through the power of the purse and appropriation of supply.

So matters stood at the accession of Edward I. The exactions of the crown were limited in the case of the chief subjects of assessment, wools, and leather and wine, but were unlimited with regard to all other merchandise. This was especially the case in the time of the French and Scotch wars, when the necessities of the crown compelled it to resort to the extreme measure of maltolte levied both in specie and kind. A climax was reached in the year 1297, when, after enduring the repeated and extortionate prises of the crown during two whole years, all classes of its subjects joined in the presentation of a statement of grievances, and supported the aristocratic movement which led to a *coup d'état*, and a solemn declaration of reform embodied in the confirmation of the charters and the articles thereto appended. From this time forward, then, the crown abandoned its rights to unconstitutional prises, and to extraordinary Customs, such as maltolte. In future, therefore, it might take for its use only such quantity of provisions as was absolutely required for the royal household. So, too, it might levy no Custom beyond the half-mark, and mark upon wools and leather, without consent of Parliament. The result of this constitutional assay was that the prerogative claimed in both directions by the crown was restored to political currency with an altered denomination in either case, and which henceforth obtained with few interruptions. The modified prise became 'purveyance,' properly limited to the requirements of the royal household, while the arbitrary maltolte, when granted by Parliament to relieve the crown's necessities, became a subsidy, levied for long after at the same rate as the imposition which it had supplanted.

The subsidy was a Parliamentary grant in excess of the Customs, levied by virtue of the crown's prerogative from certain classes of merchandise after the respective rates appointed in every case. Therefore, just as the Customs proper were of a twofold nature, so, too, were the corresponding subsidies. The ancient Custom on wools and leather was linked with a subsidy upon the same commodities, collected and answered at the same places, in the same manner, and returned in the same account as the other. The distinction between the two was this : that the Custom of wools and leather was derived from the ancient prerogative of the crown, limited and renewed in Parliament. The subsidy of wools and leather, on the other hand, depended upon the grant of Parliament, limited equally as to the rate, but unlike the other, also limited as to its duration. The second sort of subsidy was that which practically followed the details of the new Custom of the crown, imposed, strictly speaking, upon aliens only. The chief branches of this latter revenue were derived respectively from wines imported, and from cloths imported or exported, like the above, only by aliens. If we add to this list the supplementary toll in kind paid by denizens upon wines in the shape of the prisage, the new Custom of cloth paid by the same at a lower rate, and the poundage, not lawfully due, upon their goods of avoir-du-pois, but realized by the crown at its best discretion, we shall perhaps complete our examination of every article on which Custom in any shape was chargeable. According to the precedent of the original subsidy, therefore, though at an interval of thirty years, an increase of all these Customs was made by grant of Parliament. This, in its usual form, was the grant of tunnage, as a subsidy upon every tun of wine imported by denizens or aliens alike beyond the prisage and butlerage ; and that of poundage, or the subsidy payable both by denizens and aliens upon every librate of merchandise beyond the poundage already paid by aliens.

Lastly there remains to be mentioned the Parliamentary subsidies assessed on lands and goods in excess of, or rather in lieu of, the ancient feudal evies, which had become obsolete before the middle of the fourteenth century.

These, then, were the subsidies raised in the eighth year of Edward III., and continued down to our own day as the land-tax and income-tax respectively, the latter in a more rudimentary form as the tenths and fifteenths of all movables, and the former with little change either of form or title. From this time we read no more of scutages or carucages, or of halfs or fortieths. The feudal incidents alone remained an odious and obsolete liability down to the reign of Charles II., when their place was taken by the Excise, which was destined to become the mainstay of the Budgets of the eighteenth century, even as the modern form of the income-tax has proved to be in our own day.

APPENDIX.

NOTES TO THE ILLU..TRATIONS.

FRONTISPIECE.—Drawn from the original chest in the Public Record Office. A view of this chest is given in the photozinco-graph edition of Domesday Book, which, however, affords a very inadequate idea of its *contour*. This receptacle was one of many similar *Arcæ* which are described in the *Dialogus de Scaccario*, and notices of which appear throughout the ancient calendars of the treasury of the Receipt. The measurement of this chest is given at p. 50.

Fig. 1, p. 31.—Sketch-plan of the ancient Palace and Church of Westminster, showing the probable position of the Exchequer buildings and of the Tower mentioned in the *Dialogus*. The date of this theoretical plan is the thirty-first year of Edward I., subsequent, therefore, to the great fire, and the removal of the Barons' Court to the opposite side of the Great Hall. The Exchequer itself was, however, at this time temporarily fixed at York. From this time onwards the old site was occupied by the offices of the Receipt (Pells and Audit), while the Tower was eventually merged in the structure of the Chapel of St. Stephen's, used as the House of Commons. The ground-plan of the Abbey precincts is intended to illustrate the position of the treasury at the time of the robbery, and the movements of the supposed thieves.*

Fig. 2, p. 52.—Drawing of a hanaper, or hamper, used as a receptacle for loose records.

Fig. 3, p. 52.—Drawing of a skippet, or turned vase of wood, used for a like purpose.

Figs. 4 to 18, pp. 55-58.—Symbols affixed to Exchequer chests or other receptacles of records in the fourteenth and fifteenth centuries, and intended as a form of picture-writing for the purpose of describing the contents. Some of these were merely temporary in character, others more permanent, and probably utilized down to the present century. Thus there is still a wooden box preserved in the Public Record Office, and recently in use, which is marked with a star as a symbol for

---

* Since this was written, further excavations at Winchester have disclosed a considerable portion of the old Norman palace in or connected with which the Treasury was first permanently fixed at the beginning of the twelfth century. It should have been mentioned incidentally in Chapter I. that another so-called 'confession' is preserved, namely, that of J. de Rippinghall (T. of R. Misc. $\frac{2}{41}$), but it throws no light whatever on the mystery.

the Star Chamber, and some still earlier symbols are preserved on record pouches. Most of these figures explain at a glance the use they were intended to serve. They are all drawn from the originals preserved at the Public Record Office in Bishop Stapleton's Calendar and the Liber Memorandorum.

Fig. 19, p. 115.—Diagram of the Exchequer-table, showing the probable combination of the counters used by the *Calculator* to mark the state of the sheriff's account as described in the *Dialogus*, i. 3. The several items of the farm of the county are arranged here in order. The top row of figures represents the amount of the farm as ascertained from the Exactory Roll. The second row shows the sums paid into the treasury by the sheriff at Easter by tallies, and at Michaelmas in cash, respectively. The rows below this represent the several sums disbursed by the sheriff out of his farm in the king's service, and allowed by the barons. These being added to the second row, represent the state of his indebtedness thus:

```
        £        s.  d.   £   s.  d.
1. 300+20×3+14  10  6 = 374  10  6
                     ─────────────
2. 300+15  ...  ...  14    = 315 14  0
3. 20+8    ...  ...  ...   =  28  0  0
4. 12  ...  ...  ...  18   2 =  12 18  2
5. 14  ...  ...  ...  17   4 =  14 17  4
                     ─────────────
                          £371  9  6

Balance against sheriff ...  £3  1  0
```

Fig. 20, p. 121.—An Exchequer tally, drawn from the original in the Public Record Office. The Latin superscription records that 'Thomas Godesire owes to Joscy, of Kent, the Jew, 30s., namely, a half at the feast of St. Michael in the year of Grace 1229, and a half at the feast of St. Martin next following, in accordance with the chirograph—Surety, Andrew of Mikelgate.' This tally, therefore, was probably preserved in the Exchequer of the Jews.

Fig. 21, p. 121.—Another tally, also drawn from the original. The superscription is as follows : 'Against the Reeve, of Ledecumbe, for monies received of his farm to Lady Day, and of the rent to Hock-tide in the 56th year [of Henry III.], by the hands of John Squire and Ralph Hare.' Very few specimens of these early tallies now exist. The above and several others were described by the author for the Pipe Roll Society (vol. iii.), illustrated by a photographic plate of six specimens.

Figs. 22 and 23, p. 132.—Two symbols of the Exchequer, the first of which is interesting from its very early date, and the *virgæ* or columns of account partly shown on the margins. This figure is drawn from the Memoranda Roll, L.T.R., 19 Henry III. The second figure is drawn from the Liber Memorandorum.

Fig. 24, p. 163.—The gold seal of the earliest

of the three famous golden leagues always preserved in the king's treasury. This was the charter of Alphonso the Wise, of Castille, dated November 1, 1254, in favour of Prince Edward. The gold of this seal is very fine in quality, but the surface is considerably worn. The lion and castle are probably armorial emblems. A similar charter of nearly the same date, but with a leaden seal attached, is preserved in the British Museum, in the case which contains Magna Carta.

Fig. 25, p. 171.—The gold seal of the second of the golden leagues, being the bull of Pope Clement VII., dated March 5, 1524, conferring the title of Defender of the Faith on Henry VIII. The design, unlike that of the ordinary leaden *bulla* or seal, is highly ornate.

Fig. 26, p. 211.—The famous seal of Francis I., attributed by some good judges to Benvenuto Cellini, is attached to the third golden league, the Treaty of Peace and Alliance concluded between England and France in 1527. The collar on the reverse is that of the Order of St. Michael. This figure, like the two preceding ones, is drawn from the original preserved in the Public Record Office. In the fourteenth century many other 'golden leagues' were preserved in the treasury, but these three alone survived at the end of the sixteenth century.

LIST OF AUTHORITIES.*

(i.) Manuscripts :

Lord Treasurer's Remembrancer's Memoranda Rolls.

Queen's Remembrancer's Memoranda Rolls.

Great Rolls (known as Annual, Pipe, Treasurer's, or Chancellor's).

Receipt Rolls and Books (Pells or Auditor's).

Issue Rolls and Books (Pells or Auditor's).

Red Book of the Exchequer.

Black Book of the Exchequer.

Small Black Book of the Exchequer.

Libri Munimentorum.

Originalia Rolls.

Close Rolls.

Patent Rolls.

Treasury of the Receipt Miscellanea.

* The bibliography of the Exchequer is so extensive and so widely distributed, that a complete list would form a work to itself. The present list, however, will be found to contain all the authorities required for practical purposes.

(*i.*) *Manuscripts* (continued) :
  Queen's Remembrancer's Miscellanea.
  State Papers Domestic.
  Treasury Papers.

(*ii.*) *Printed Works :*
  Madox—History and Antiquities of the
    Exchequer, 1769, 2 vols.
  Thomas—The Ancient Exchequer, 1848,
    1 vol.
  Devon—Issues of the Exchequer (Record
    Publications, No. 57).
  Vernon—The Exchequer opened, 1661,
    1 vol.
  Historical View of the Court of Ex-
    chequer, by a late Learned Judge, 1738,
    1 vol.
  Treatise on the Court of Exchequer, by a
    late Lord Chief Baron, 1758, 1 vol.
  Palgrave—Calendars and Inventories of
    the Exchequer (Record Publications,
    No. 53).
  Printed Pipe Rolls in Record Publications,
    and Pipe Roll Society's Publications.
  Jones—Index to the Memoranda and
    Originalia.
  Liebermann—Einleitung in den Dialogus
    (Gottingen), 1875.

15

(ii.) Printed Works (continued) :

　　Pike—History of Crime (Longman's), 2 vols.

　　Cunningham—Growth of Industry and Commerce, 1890, 1 vol.

　　Stubbs—Constitutional History, vols. 1 and 2.

The subject has been treated by the Author in the *Introduction to the Pipe Rolls* (Pipe Roll Society), *Court Life under the Plantagenets* (1890), and in a number of articles contributed at intervals during the last ten years to various journals.